JOSEF JEDLIČKA
MIDWAY UPON THE JOURNEY
OF OUR LIFE

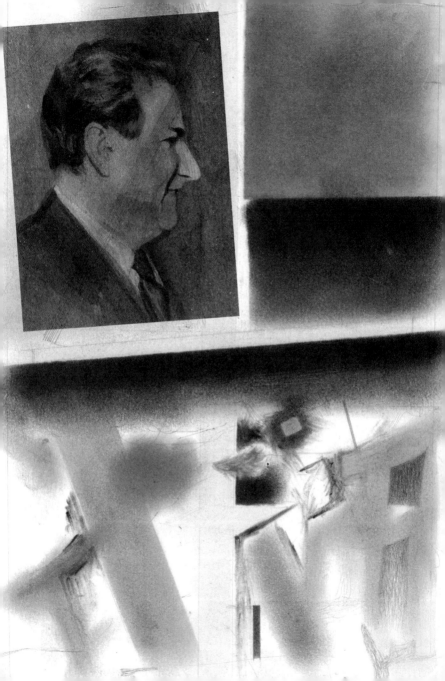

MODERN CZECH CLASSICS

Josef Jedlička
Midway Upon
the Journey of Our Life

Translated from the Czech by Alex Zucker

Karolinum Press

KAROLINUM PRESS, Ovocný trh 3–5, 116 36 Prague 1, Czech Republic
Karolinum Press is a publishing department of Charles University in Prague
www.karolinum.cz

Cover and graphic design by Zdeněk Ziegler
Typeset by DTP Karolinum
Printed in the Czech Republic by Těšínské papírny, s. r. o., Český Těšín
First English edition

Translated with the support of the Banff International Literary Translation
Centre (BILTC) at The Banff Centre, Banff, Alberta, Canada.

ISBN 978-80-246-3127-1 (hb)
ISBN 978-80-246-3128-8 (ebk)

I

WE CAN BEGIN AND END anywhere, for we have not made a pact with victory, but with struggle. In the old days they began with childhood — yet how many mass graves have they filled in since then! What a terrible burden of vigilant loyalty has accrued to us over the years, what an effort we make to bear its weight, so we may still be capable of hope and love today, and, perhaps, again tomorrow!

But I am writing a book: *Somewhere in the middle of life comes a moment when a man must take his fate into his own hands.* For it comes to pass that the young woman we hope for from birth and remember to our final hour marries and gives birth to a child. You kissed her just once, in the rain, on a street corner, with the perfume of heroic lilacs still in the air. The child of course is a boy. And he looks like you, *he looks like you!* — your spitting image. And it comes to pass that they kill a poet before your eyes and a weary policeman, a gentle soul, brings home a sheet of paper from an unfinished piece

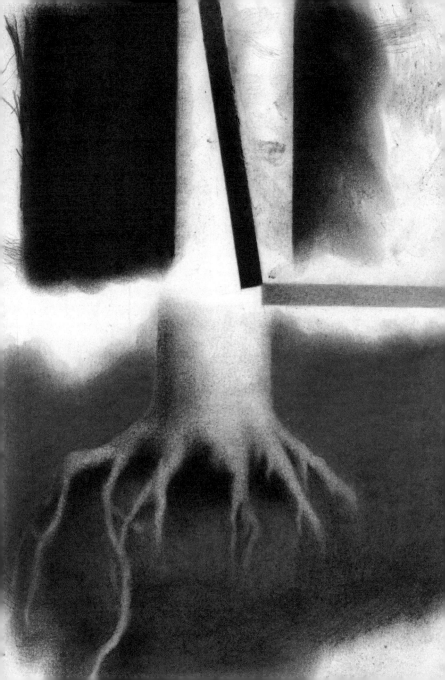

of writing, folded into a fortune teller for his children. And then it comes to pass one day that tender young seamstresses, their doll-like busts working in graceful rhythm, put in overtime to mend the red banner of the revolution using the finest thread. And that is that moment. It usually comes before sunup, and from that point on, lyricism is done for.

LYRIC POETRY — as everyone knows — differs from epic poetry in that it doesn't tell stories: its stories are hidden. But even back then I yielded to it only as a vice, in those first years after February, encased in wooden scaffolding — while she was still asleep . . . Afterward you end up with a pounding headache, sick to your stomach, but to miss out on your first love is something that stays with you all your life. So there can be no more lyricism. The essence of lyricism is the decanonization of themes, in other words, a muddle. Freedom, they say! But who will be our witness when the day comes, who, when we are completely and definitively alone?!

As for method, the method of prose is deceleration and the method of poetry is semantic reversal. Thus men slow down and women want to be done as quickly as possible. But that's just it, there's not enough freedom. We live in a man's world, the methodological and semantic context of prose, established and reestablished over and over, ad nauseam, by way of awkward digressions. Of course. There were women who trained to be locksmiths and train engineers, so nobody writes prose on a whim. No one knows how it will all turn out. And in prose, you can end anywhere: "So that, when I stretched out my hand, I caught hold of the *fille de chambre*'s –" The end. Or he dies.

I WILL BEGIN, THEN, with my state of siege. Every two hundred yards along the road that leads from the Stalin Works to the Collective House in Litvínov, there is a date inscribed in the concrete. Behind the old slaughterhouse, amid a group of unplastered brick buildings constructed by French POWs during the war, worn by rain and sticky with sulfurous ash from the factories and open-pit mines, is the date 18. II. 1948. A little higher up, in the direction of the future, a child's bare footprints are pressed into the concrete.

Long before they took us prisoner here in these model family homes, there was nothing beyond this but fallow land, pitted with bomb craters, and a few lone huts of rotting black plank, some forgotten groves of birch, barbed wire, tissue paper roses dotting the grass pink and blue — and on the site where my bookshelf now stands, a wild rabbit had its nest.

Back then we still walked the streets of Prague quietly singing an old Russian revolutionary song into the night, the one Lenin supposedly whistled, leaning against the ledge of the open window that misty November morning in the hush of the long pause before the *Aurora* fired off its famous shot. Someone had adapted it to local circumstances, changing the refrain to "Lidice–Most–Litvínov . . ."

The Youth Union brigades had begun building homes and were doing a pretty bad job of it. Most of the walls didn't meet at a right angle, so it was difficult to set up the wardrobes and beds when we moved in one November day — by that same fatal logic that in the end always convinces you that no word and no name can be taken in vain.

They were building in a hurry. There wasn't time.

We recited Mayakovsky to taciturn landholders, owners of an acre or half an acre, in pubs that served weak beer, and most of the girls that summer lost their sad wartime virginity — for disappointment and grief were far, far in the future, and the murky dawns were only just beginning to collect, imperceptibly, in a slender strand of the first gray hair.

The doors didn't close properly either, and would open on their own, thudding in the draft. To this day the neighborhood resounds with muffled banging on windy days, an organic sound, like the roar of surf or the hum of a forest. The countryside has yet to adapt itself to the city. A few years ago there was a thicket of beech right behind the house, you could just pop out from the kitchen and a few minutes later be gathering mushrooms for soup among the electric cables and tin cans and baby carriage skeletons. It was no longer like that by the time we arrived, because the children had trampled down the mycelium and the forest soil had been covered over with humus after the last battle was won and people were finally authorized to have gardens.

AT FIRST THEY HAD IN MIND a uniform layout for the grounds around the blocks of flats. Back then most people still didn't have any sense of the difference in principle between Breton and socialist realism; back then, when this housing estate was being built, we all still believed in Rilke and free love.

So any individual modifications were prohibited. Inspections, unscheduled and unannounced, threatened severe consequences for anyone who violated the public nature of the space. Yet there were still many broken bricks, planks, cables, scraps of wire mesh, and the wind, which blows where it will, sowed haphazardly an aster here, a marigold there, so there was uncertainty right from the start as to what was actually intentional and what was not. Men with armbands on their sleeves stood in befuddlement over stray clumps of purple columbine and silently beat their way through the bushes of black elder — anxiously wondering whether they might be betraying the cause of the working class.

Yet for a long time nobody dared. Only on dark, starless nights did they sneak out in front of the building with children's shovels, glancing around in alarm at the distant whoop of drunkards and the yowl of mating cats, planting radishes, parsley, and chives in the damp corners sheltered by the brickwork terraces. The children of course pilfered it, and this violation of discipline and the collectivist spirit was the topic of frequent heated debates at plenary sessions of the Party's local organs.

In the context of the struggle against formalism, as well as perhaps in recognition of economic necessity, people used low wire fencing to stake out household gardens in irregular rectangular plots.

Now it was time for enrichment. The earth was dry and rocky, and dug up by bulldozers, even hen and chicks barely took hold in it. People pushed baby carriages a mile and a half loaded with pails and baskets full of fertile soil. Our neighbor claimed to have trucked in seven hundred and thirty-six loads of forest dirt. He found his site in a hollow where some foxes used to have their den. The earth there was heavy, and rich in ammonia due to the rotting carcasses of baby

hares and mice and golden-plumed birds, and perhaps even a man shot down on the run. The furious growth of the peonies still brings to light a fragile little white bone every now and then.

So it was that everyone settled in, growing thick and putting out branches; so it was that we moved into the city under siege.

OUR NEIGHBOR THE VIGILANT outpost works in the garden all day long, to the point that in the summer it seems he hardly sleeps. I run into him at six thirty a.m. as he returns home from the night shift.

"Good night," I say, according to local custom, as he lays his briefcase down on a bench beneath a truncated tree and roots around in the dirt, yanking up weed sprouts.

"Good night!" he replies guardedly, and I lower my eyes so he won't catch me, so he won't see that I know how irrevocably, how desperately irrevocably the rosy day arising above the dark hills fills the vale of May. And as I walk away, he sinks into reverie, gazing down on his little rock garden and beds of kohlrabi and onion.

I return in the afternoon to find him hard at work. He is transplanting some delicate young plants from a hotbed he built with his own hands with the help of his late brother-in-law, and at day's end he handles the watering hose with the meticulous precision of a calligrapher. His voice is soft, with a cultivatedly cruel diction. "The primrose," he says, "otherwise known as the primula, comes in many varieties. One would never have imagined. So for instance you have the *Primula pruhoniciana*, the 'Springtime' primula, distinguished, as you see, by its pink notched petals, the dwarf primrose, the summer primrose, the purple . . . well, at any rate, I could go on and on, it's something of a hobby of mine. The way some people like a drink or two out on the town. True, there's always work to be done, but the boy does appreciate a taste of strawberries now and then, even if it's only a few."

Our own garden lies fallow.

"That's good black earth you've got right there, just waiting to be dug," he says to me sometimes with a look nothing escapes.

He was a policeman before the war. I don't like police, I don't like living under police surveillance.

"We saw plenty of their sort in our day," the policeman said one evening, lighting half a cigarette in a long cherrywood holder. "Hussies! But the men on the force, we knew how to handle them. We had this little implement, the spike we called it, like this, up our sleeve. And they came with us, yes sir. They came right along, like lambs. There were times — I'm telling you —

the things we saw, it was like a novel. Yes sir, a novel, only not the kind they write." Then, having defined his poetics, he resumed: "This one time with my partner, Husárek — you remember him, hon, good-looking guy! — this one time we pulled a raid on this . . . one of these little hideaway joints. Busted in there, wham bam. You know, the usual, booze, cards — but one of the hussies, she wasn't having it. Uh-uh, did not want to go. She bit, scratched. Little minx. So to teach her a lesson, as they say, we took her in as is. Just like that, in her birthday suit. Nothing but her high heels. That was the year of the big frost, when the trees froze over. By the time we got her to the station, she'd turned white as a ghost on us."

Then the light went out. Power loss. That happened often. The policeman sat smoking, feeling indulgent toward the world because summer was turning to fall and he already had his crocus, hyacinth, and tulip bulbs stored away in the cellar. A cold wind was beginning to blow from Siberia, reeking of tar and the smoke of furtive fires. There were still men in concentration camps standing for night roll call. We listened tensely to the doors' muffled banging, no one said a word. Then I went home and ate my cold dinner with my hands alone in the dark, because the shops were out of candles and it had been nine months since Christmas.

AT NINE THE ALARM CLOCKS start going off. Rise and shine for the night shift. Most of the children are already asleep. The women are coming home from the shops and canteens. In the doorway they share a fleeting kiss with their husbands, who smell of sweat, coal dust, and hydrogen sulfide.

I sit with my sticky fingers spread, watching the wintering flies settle onto them, and ponder the fact that there is barely coal for a week in the cellar. On the other side of the wall someone is playing Tchaikovsky's *1812 Overture* on an old raspy gramophone. Suddenly the door opens and in walks a woman wearing my mother's wedding dress, a bouquet of Parma violets pinned to her bosom, with fishnet gloves and white leather boots. In her outstretched left hand she holds a blue porcelain candelabra ablaze with sallow tapers that singe a loose red lock of her hair with a sizzling crackle.

With a single abrupt gesture, graceful yet just hurried enough that it leaves a red scratch on her throat, she opens her dress and her tanned breasts slip out of the fine Valenciennes lace.

"We brought you some coal," she says, beckoning me to follow her.

"It's still a week till payday," I say.

"Not to worry, *mon cher!*" She presses my face to her warm, blue-veined breasts. "Poor Count de Lérouville is footing the bill, of course."

So I walk out in front of the house and pour my last coins into the black-stained palm of the old wagonman: "Careful, friend, you don't want to soil the lady's dress!" The coal is deposited in front of the house: a big beautiful walnut of high heating value. The woman in the 1924 wedding dress lays the bouquet of violets on top of the heap and walks away. She walks away: "*Adieu!*" And as she turns to glance back one last time, the chill white of her throat shines from the furs around her neck. Meanwhile the "Marseillaise" is drowned out in the thunder of bells from the Cathedral of the Annunciation in the Kremlin. And after that, nothing but silence, a whooshing void untouched by even the most distant memory of applause at the Prague Spring concert in '48 where one of my old friends lent me an uncensored copy of *The State and Revolution.* Then Páleníček performed the "Appassionata."

The door opens by itself. I am tense, as though at any moment I might be caught in the act, once and for all. And the dark stream flows on through the factory gate, the loudspeakers blare a marching tune, the punch clocks ding, a red star shines above the cooling tower, and gray buses filled with prisoners quietly drive through the gate next door. We all wake to a shapeless night with the obstinate courage of despair, as if the dawn were never to come again. The workers begin their shift.

I'M NOT THE ONE CREATING the context. I'm writing an encyclopedia, giving testimony, hiding from the searching gaze of the policeman, in plain view of the world, on the second floor of this ramshackle building that any key can unlock. The point hasn't been to interpret the world for some time now. The only thing that matters at the moment is fate. I am who I am — and you, you are the only ones I can call as my witnesses: you, men rocking a car on the clutch in the middle of a hill, you, stripped to the waist, giving a cheer as you bury gas pipe in the ground, you, women with old lady's bellies, lining up for meat at five o'clock in the morning, you, starving, beaten, and tortured, coughing up the last drops of blood on the concrete bunkers' moldy floors, you, drunken boasters formerly on a first-name basis with Frištenský the wrestler, you, technicians trained in the factories of Škoda and Siemens, earning a *Brandenburg Concerto* in a single man-hour — you, men with whom one day, it seems, one way or another, I will charge the bayonet side by side.

But who today can judge? Whose fault it is that we have forsaken each other? Who cast this spell on us that, sitting over a glass of beer, we read each other's lips like the deaf for the lost words of fraternity and solidarity? To what beginnings previous to other beginnings must we return to rediscover a mutually intelligible code for the morning mist and the felled tree, for the swoop of a bird in flight, for the silence in a darkness teeming with little owls and barn owls?

Back in those days, in the age of innocence and hope, I lived in Prague with two sisters, the younger of whom, years later, I married. She still believed in those days that the cast-iron wheel with the handle in the operator's cabin was what steered the tramway cars, clear evidence of how we unintentionally strip the world of its potential miraculousness with lyricism. The small flat was constantly full of people, coming and going as they pleased, since we kept the key under the mat. Cigarettes were still rationed, so we smoked them one at a time, passing them around the table and stuffing the butts into paper holders for later. We sat around the fold-up sewing machine till daylight, debating transition classes according to Marx and "The Part Played by Labor in the Transition from Ape to Man." Also sexual issues and monogamy. We attended lectures, as long as they didn't start too early in the morning, and locked ourselves in the bathroom to cram before exams. Whenever we had any loose change, it went into a common pool, so every now and then we could get drunk on fruit wine, 46 old-currency crowns a bottle. Sometimes we drank rubbing alcohol with grapefruit juice: The med students supplied the spirits, the juice came courtesy of the UNRRA.

Couples went into the entryway to neck. And then sometimes, toward morning, gone soft with fatigue and the sweet and ineffable certainty of God's just kingdom, as the blackbirds out in the courtyard began to screech, we serenaded the stain-covered wall on the building across the way with "The Internationale."

A milkman and his wife lived in the flat next door to us. Quiet, modest, considerate folk. The wife, tiny with black eyes, was pregnant, and sometimes she would come over to ask us for an aspirin. She contributed to our debates on Bertrand Russell without realizing it by showing off her blue layette to the girls. But then late one night she ended up giving birth to a little girl while I was shooting out the window at the wall across the way with a Belgian 9mm left behind in our flat by the Germans.

They weren't so strict about firearms licenses in those days, despite the official position that *arms in the hands of the people gave rise to tensions*.

EARLY FEBRUARY WAS warm, with conditions particularly favorable for sighting a white horse be-

tween the fences, legs spattered black by the surface of an autumnal lake, or Icarus thrashing among the birches in Rieger Gardens. People stood long past midnight, overcoats unbuttoned, quarreling and arguing and debating on the sidewalk in front of the Melantrich building. We opened the windows at nighttime, enjoying the cool feel of the air on our naked bodies.

During those same days, somebody spat on a Czechoslovak Communist Party display case, just up the street from the Vinohrady market hall. The neighborhood agitprop committee framed the spit in blue glazier's pencil and wrote in big letters: THIS IS HOW THE ENEMIES OF THE NATION AND THE WORKING CLASS FIGHT! It was clear that something had to happen, the time was ripe. Besides — we were the youth of the world.

Some of the people who came to see us in those days were Čestmír J., who went on to study medicine and I'm told now works at the psychiatric hospital in Bohnice; Miloš P., a German-looking blond with a German sense of order — for that matter he also had a German name — who even then already knew a lot about nuclear physics and relay computers; Dáša H., a very beautiful and very sad architect, whom years later I would bump into carrying blueprints for arched lintels, Corinthian capitals, and Byzantine colonnades; Vít Č., who no one yet knew would become an informer; Honza, refined and brilliant, with a personality so transparent he could barely be discerned by the naked eye, and his brother, the little boy who was ultimately destined to take the stand for Balzac, and Slávek M., the one who loaned me the uncensored edition of Lenin and who, having achieved the rank of doctor of philosophy, inherited from his father a working automobile; and Milan and a something or other Kuňa, and Irena and Božka and Fíma and Hanka and Soňa, and another ten or so whose names and faces I'm slowly forgetting . . .

Besides me and the two sisters studying medicine, we also had a subletter in the flat and, sometimes, K. the med student. The subletter, a former nun who had run away from the novitiate, would come home around eleven at night, fill the bath with hot water, and sit there steaming, hair up in a pink net, practicing her stenography on news briefs from *Tvorba*, the cultural review.

K. the med student, meanwhile, would spend whole days just sitting in front of the gramophone. We didn't have too many records: "Rue de la Gaîté" by Nezval and Burian; "Ol' Man River," sung by Paul Robeson; "Sentimental Journey," which wasn't so associated with Viktor Shklovsky yet in those days; "Kanava," a Russian folk song; Ravel's *Boléro*; part of the third movement of Mozart's Concerto in D Minor; and the Jewish prayer "El Malei Rachamim," recorded by a Bulgarian or Romanian cantor named Katz, the only one to be saved right out of the gas chamber. Whenever he wasn't asleep, the med student sat by the gramophone silently, and while the rest of us argued, pacing around the little room and pounding our fists on the sewing machine that served as our table, again and again he would play that despondent Jewish prayer, which at one point breaks into an Oriental-sounding falsetto chant. As soon as the record finished, he would very slowly rewind the device, change the needle, take his allotted three drags off the cigarette, and start the record over again from the beginning.

The day the Litvínov child left his footprints in the road's concrete, the newspapers carried the news of the government's resignation. It turned chilly and a damp snow began to fall. We went out into the streets of Prague and walked the city, heads held high, red stars on our lapels.

On the impassioned steps of the Rudolfinum, shivering in a light spring jacket, a young girl sat folding a paper airplane. In the great auditorium of the Philosophical Faculty, a Social Democrat gave a slap in the face to a short, lewd National Socialist, who even during lectures on Husserl's *Logical Investigations* slipped references to his sexual problems into the discussion.

Maybe two days later, they called a meeting of the Party's university committee at the Slovanský dům. We were advised to be on the alert. There was talk of a general strike and they were checking people's IDs. A young editor from the Party daily *Rudé právo* stood on a chair in the back of the large low-ceilinged hall, speaking with his shoulder thrust forward. His coveralls were so new they hadn't even been washed. Someone there told me a young poet had demanded to be let on national radio to perform his poem "We Recite Death" for the people. They denied him partly on principle and partly because he couldn't trill his r's properly.

By the time we came home it was very late. K. the med student was listening to "El Malei Rachamim," and sitting on the couch next to him was a miner from Most named Joska, who was courting my future sister-in-law. To judge from the way he was bragging about his motorcycle exploits and the fact that he slept with an open knife beneath his pillow, he was very much in love with her. We informed him that the revolution was probably going to start the next day.

"Is that right?" he said, giving me a slap on the shoulder. "Hey, college boy, I'll bet you can't even ride a moped down a flight of stairs. I can and I've got a big bike, we're talking DKW 500. OHV!"

We were thrilled to have him, and I shared in the excitement, since in those difficult days even the mere presence of a true representative of the working class was encouraging. I happily settled in on an improvised bed of couch pillows, and later that night the radio announced that Gottwald was going to speak on Old Town Square the next day. Joska and my sister-in-law were still leaning out the window sharing a cigarette when I fell asleep. They were talking about the shafts and open-pit mines here in the north, where they had met, about Most and Růžodol, about Komořany and Ervěnice, about the sites of my destiny that I had yet to glimpse, about gigantic conveyors towering over a barren range of slag heaps, the artificial landscape of my life, the world in its original form or finished once and for all, little by little, bit by bit, devouring everything.

THE WORKERS' BARRACKS stand arrayed around the factory and perched along the edges of the gaping open-pit mines. The buildings are left over from the German concentration camps. Around 1950 some were returned to their original purpose, while others were modified for use as family housing or lodging for volunteer work brigades. Two sets of two rooms with a small shared entryway, then they carried out a general disinfection and set up a dispensary for treatment of venereal disease. Many brigade workers had ended up getting married here, and social relations were increasingly shaped by family life.

This year, on the occasion of the February anniversary, the miners received a bonus. The red banners drooped in the sleet the way they had back in '48, and Joska the miner's switchblade — Joska who I heard ended up marrying the daughter of a Slovak wine distiller — had been gathering rust under the eaves for years now.

František Pomykal used the money from his bonus to buy his family an electric washing machine. There was a line in front of the shop, but they got what they had come for. They used a child's wagon to cart it home through the sleet, man in front, women and children pushing from behind. The children were so excited, they crashed the wagon into the wall, giving the washer a scrape.

"No big deal," Pomykal said. "Kids. What can you do? I'll touch it up tomorrow. It'll be just like new. The motor's what counts. You don't buy a washer for show. And the motor runs like a dream, I can tell you that much."

His neighbor Josef Sviták helped them get it into the building, while the Pomykal children stuck out their tongues at the kids next door, chanting: "Na-na na-na na-na! We've got a new Perota!"

The next-door neighbor cuffed her children on the head as they looked on mutely, passive and helpless, then couldn't resist chiming in herself: "Looks kinda scraped!"

"Sometimes you really do get lucky in life!" said Pomykal's wife as they installed the machine in the corner next to the stove. "There were a good sixty of us and just eleven washers."

They still had to extend the cord and adjust the contact. The fuses blew a few times, but finally the machine started up. They stood watching in silent amazement.

Pomykal squatted on his haunches, switching the washer on and off. Sviták listened, facing the window.

"I'd say it knocks!" he remarked.

"Well, you'd be wrong," said Pomykal. "It runs like clockwork." Still, he took a step back and lowered his head with a look of concentration on his face. Outside, the red banners flapped against the flagpoles. "I can tell when a washer knocks!" he said after a moment.

"Whatever you say," Sviták said, walking out without a good-bye.

That night the Pomykal family practically didn't eat, switching the washer on and off until nearly midnight. The father got up every now and then to stretch his legs. The two youngest children fell asleep on the floor.

Morning came and Pomykal left for work. Sviták had the afternoon shift, but he hadn't been able to sleep well during the night, so he got dressed while it was still dark and sat with his elbows propped on the table, a cigarette between his fingers.

His wife, barely awake, said from under the covers: "You suck those things down all day long. One after the other."

Sviták ignored her, staring gloomily into the empty corner next to the range.

After a while his wife, moaning and groaning, got out of bed, turned on the radio and, still in her night-shirt, went to the faucet to fill the washpot. "It's me, me, young liberty, a red-petaled flower, blossoming free," Rudolf Cortés sang. "Look at Pomykal!" Svitáková shouted over the water tanging against the metal. "Look at him! You don't see him smoking!"

"Pomykal," Sviták muttered. "Yeah, well, Pomykal can kiss my . . ."

"Because it's true," his wife said illogically, setting the pot on the stove. Her breasts, large and swollen underneath her soaked nightshirt, flopped against her drooping belly.

Her husband slowly stamped out his cigarette and turned away toward the window, where, outside, clumps of damp snow floated in the first morning light. "There's a new operator on the hoist at the fourth incline," he said with spite in his voice. "Damn good woman, hard as coal."

"Everyone, you hear me, everyone's got a Perota nowadays!" His wife collapsed, crying, onto a chair. "Coal!" she sobbed. "Everyone's got one, even the gypsies!"

"Stop your blubbering," Sviták said. He buttoned up his shirtsleeves, crossed through the shared entryway, and stepped into the neighbors' space without knocking.

Pomykal's wife was heating a bottle of milk for the baby.

Ennobled by her new possession, she chided the children clustered around the washing machine: "Don't you know how to say hello?"

Sviták slammed the door. "I thought so," he said. "That would suit you, wouldn't it? Stuffing your belly off the sweat of the working class!"

He shoved the woman out of the way and in two long strides he was at the machine.

"Are you crazy?" Pomykalová shouted, but Sviták had already yanked the plug out of the wall and kicked over the washer. As the children, screaming, threw themselves at his legs, their mother jumped in and ripped open the shirt on his back.

"If I say it knocks," Sviták roared, stomping up and down on the machine, "then by God Almighty it knocks!"

Pomykalová bit and scratched, but Sviták hit her in the head and, brandishing the poker, he rasped: "I'm going to smash this whole place to smithereens! Nobody, and I mean nobody, is going to tell me whether or not a motor knocks!"

His wife, drawn by the commotion, entered in a flowery robe to find the Pomykal family rolling on the ground in a pool of blood while Sviták pounded the washer into a shapeless lump. The other neighbors came running as well.

"Yep," said a woman cradling an infant in her arms. "Like I always say, no tree grows to heaven."

"I've got nothing against giving a broad a slap or two from time to time, but a machine, now that's something else!" commented an older man, turning his back on the scene.

Svitáková stepped toward the wall with a determined look in her eye and tore down a photograph of her and Pomykalová standing side by side in a group of young girls, a souvenir from the days when they were still single and practiced gymnastics routines together at the Red Trade Unions academy. In the process she overturned the pot on the stove.

"Look, oxtail!" cried the woman from the building across the way. "Can you believe it? I wonder where they dug that up? I haven't seen any oxtail for a good year and a half."

"How much you willing to pay, ma'am?" a pimpled adolescent grinned — and everyone burst out laughing, while Svitáková tore off the tablecloth and trampled on the comforters, sending feathers slowly circling through the air.

Finally two men tore Sviták away from the machine. "The parts aren't worth a tinker's dam!" said one of them, pocketing the rotor on the sly. Meanwhile another neighbor called the medical center, since there were wounded and since calling a doctor is standard practice when people don't know what else to do. There were still feathers floating in the air when the ambulance arrived with a young female practitioner who dressed the wounds and drew up the medical certificates attesting to bodily harm.

DAY BROKE and the loudspeakers lining the streets began broadcasting a program to mark the anniversary of the February revolution. It gave you the feeling that on any corner you might stumble upon a thousand-headed throng, past mingling with present in a disturbing *illusion de déjà vu*. It was raining like it had been then, back in '48, but the street was de-

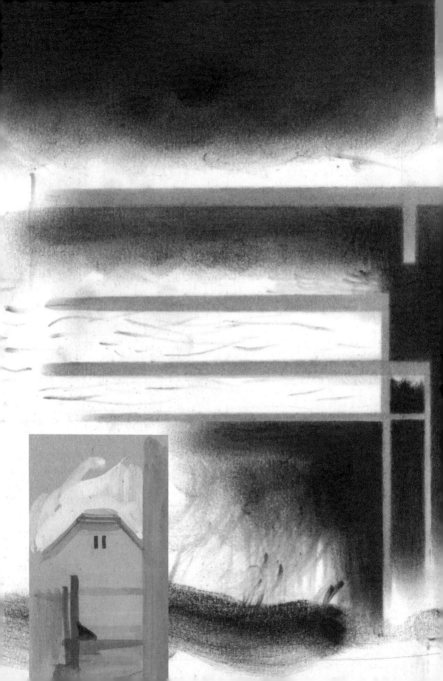

serted except for some trash men banging trash cans around.

It was Gottwald speaking, a recording of his speech on Old Town Square. His voice kept fading out, lost in the rising cries of the enormous crowd. I listened closely, in the hope that I might recognize the past of my own voice, but my listening was in vain. Public expressions of jubilation had yet to be refined and our cries were for the most part inarticulate.

We stood there in front of Kinský Palace bareheaded, hands in our pockets, as a somber crowd flooded the square from the surrounding streets: metal workers and machinists from the ČKD and Ringhoffer factories, munitions workers from the Žižkov cartridge company, bashful men with briefcases and forty-something-year-old men with the air of frightened chickens and a future of district school inspector written on their foreheads. A few girls in national costume, according to the custom established in '45, clambered up onto the rain-soaked monument to Jan Hus. The lights blazed in the tall windows of the insurance company, where men and women sat hunched over their typewriters and calculators, tirelessly pecking away. The manager of the tavern next door to the Štorch House had a table set up in the passageway in front of the taproom, offering tea and frankfurters for sale.

Gottwald appeared amid a small coterie on the balcony of the palace, directly above the grilled windows from which Franz Kafka once contemplated the Marian Column. The shouts and cheers that now carried through the deserted street with the banging trashcans were accompanied by the waving of banners and standards. A wet snow fell as Gottwald began his speech.

Suddenly we realized the moment was historic. The speaker's appearance was accentuated with a Persian lamb hat, in an obvious attempt to set the moment apart from the everyday order of things. The era of flat caps was drawing to a close and the age of brimmed hats was dawning: The lamb hat guaranteed a smooth transition. He had never worn one before and would never wear one again.

He spoke in a deep, faltering voice, restarting some sentences three or four times, while we stood there, below the balcony, chanting slogans, squeezed between men in blue coveralls, trying in vain to adjust our indoor voices to match the screams of the women in red scarves, who would later play such an important role in the ethnography of the May Day parades' joyous optimism. Wispy flakes of snow melted on our glowing cheeks as we lifted our faces to see. A flock of doves frantically circled the towers of Týn Church, little suspecting the wicker baskets in which they would be jailed too many times to count over the coming years as a tangible demonstration of the ideas of freedom and peace. Today I can no longer find the pathos in that moment. Perhaps there was none. All that remains of it for me now is an unsettling burnt smell, a reminder of the feeling that comes over me whenever I'm squeezed into the middle of a crowd, a subconscious fear of being trampled to death in a panic. The psychiatric term for it, I believe, is claustrophobia.

"I'm afraid of being buried alive," a friend of mine often says. "I'm going to have an electric buzzer installed in my grave."

"It's birth trauma," says my wife. "Everyone has it."

A poet friend chimes in with a motif of the pastoral novel: "Once, near where we live, they exhumed a grave and found the deceased lying in the coffin with his face to the bottom and all his fingers chewed to the bone. Not to mention that countess from Brno with her head gracefully tilted, just so."

"Schopenhauer," says another, "put in his will that he couldn't be buried until his body showed clear signs of decomposition."

"Schopenhauer of course being the last word in European philosophy," adds yet another, whose wife is in her eighth month. "From there we move to deeds: by which of course I mean Auschwitz, Majdanek, and Katyń."

As for me, I say nothing, anxiously dismissing the thought of the most terrifying story I know, Kafka's diary entry about two children, alone in their home, who climbed into a large trunk, shut the lid behind them, and suffocated to death.

So Gottwald has delivered his speech and now, in the thickening rain of myth, the final battle cries are sounded to the jubilant hordes, many of whom have surely been visited since that day by death on its silent advance toward this rainy day of a higher-order reality. The banners hang limply on the rain-soaked flagpoles, and in the barracks overlooking the smoking chasm of the open-pit mine, a snow-white feather of down still circles above the stove.

A brisk march rings out from the streetside loudspeakers. It's a new spring for socialism.

There were a few other speakers after Gottwald that day. We had a chance to hear Jan Drda, in a rainproof jacket, and a member of Parliament from the Social Democrats, wearing a beret.

"That one sure doesn't look like she just switched sides yesterday," remarked a man in the crowd in front of Kinský Palace." Everywhere, comrades, I'm telling you, we had our people everywhere!

This was long before the female trainees at the mining school in Schönbach near Litvínov started wearing

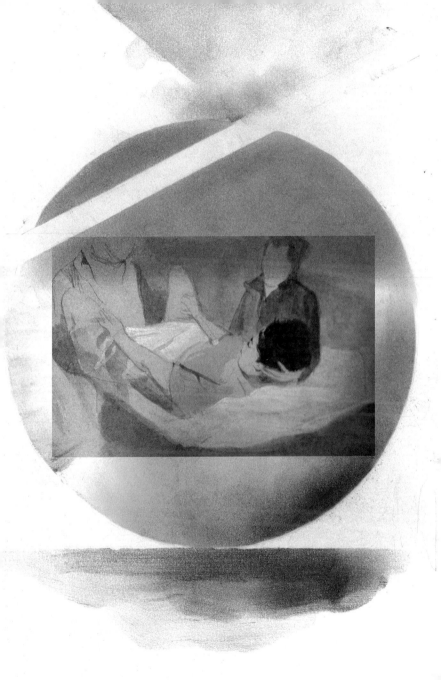

their hair cropped short, that is, long before they saw Lucia Bosè on the silver screen. There were still posters for the Social Democrats plastered around Prague with a picture of the Tower of London and the slogan "Our banner waves over thrones," and by a strange oversight, a photo of Clara Zetkin in a tie and striped blouse still adorned the walls of some workers' clubhouses.

We returned home that February day soaking wet and excited. As usual, K. the medical student, who later went on to become a prominent Party functionary in one of the border regions, was sitting at the gramophone, playing "El Malei Rachamim." Joska the miner from Komořany was brewing him a cup of tea and had a plate of warm garlic bread waiting for us.

As Petr Zenkl drove off to his friends' for a pig roast, an arrogant smile plastered on his foolish face, my friend, now long lost in the caustic ash of years, paged through an album of family photographs with his first love, the child who left the prints of his little bare feet in the concrete in the middle of the old section of Litvínov was delirious with fever, Gottwald cruised the streets of Prague in an armored limousine, and a wild rabbit shivered with cold in the corner of my unfinished room.

The era of capitalism had come to an end and a new social order, a socialist order, was installed in its place.

IT'S GOING ON EIGHT YEARS NOW and I'm getting old. I wouldn't recognize you by your perfume anymore, and it's easier this way. I've gotten used to myself. I've forgotten your address, and besides, they changed the street names anyway — it's easier this way. It's going on eight years now and here I sit along the route that leads from past to future, more alone than the wild rabbit shivering with dread in the constant draft that flips back and forth through my books and sends my papers flying. What good is lyrical motivation to me here? Nonsense! Never again, never again will you switch on the red light in the last window of the house across the way by batting your eyelids, never again, my sweet, presently past, will you perilously dangle a worn-out shoe over the river as the laundrywomen gather the laundry in the twilight — and it's easier this way. Yes, easier, my dear.

I hear you have a child, a little boy. They put Pioneer bandanas in layette sets now, and my son will also be a Communist Pioneer one day, my love! Yes, it's easier when a person grows old along with the times. It's going on eight years now — comrade! Rarely does one find a bouquet of Parma violets on a pile of coal. And what good is it, anyway? What good is it wasting hard currency?

THEY USED HARD CURRENCY TO BUY two Italian trolleybuses right after '48. Articulated buses, the two halves joined by a canvas accordion, with electric resistors heating the interior all year around. The passengers stand elbow to elbow, four across, facing the direction of travel. That was how I traveled here, along a dusty road lined with tree stumps. "And like the swimmer who, having saved himself from the storm-tossed seas, looks back into the waves and feels a new terror, my soul too, though hastening toward salvation, kept glancing back into the pass from which none yet had emerged alive."

A swarm of children hollered and jumped around the stop at the end of the line, trampling down the last blades of yellow grass. A short way off, some workers dug a ditch, others rolled a gigantic boulder, and still others squatted on their haunches in front of the open hood of a truck, staring intently at the engine. I was hungry and I was choking on the stench of hydrogen sulfide that lay over the smoky fields. The local radio blasted out a marching tune on the loudspeakers. *So this is the center of the world. From here it's the same distance in every direction!*

The sun stood directly overhead. I leaned against the blackened stump of a tree, draped with paper streamers left to rot there since the First of May. The tree was a remnant of the deep forest that twenty years ago still stretched deep into the interior. They say there were once wild boar here, rooting through the fallen beech leaves, does scampering across the bright glades at night. Miners switched on their headlamps to cut through the woods to work. Smugglers carried sugar, razor blades, women's lingerie, cigarettes, and chocolate. On payday there was eating, drinking, and dancing, in every other home there was someone who played accordion or zither, and in one of every three, an anarchist. There were amateur theater performances, new Czech schools and Sokol gymnastics clubs and Red Trade Unions and restaurants for weekend tourists. And there were strikes, and there was hunger and poverty, and there were glorious May Day parades, and there was shooting into the crowd . . .

I didn't know all that yet in the summer of '53. I only found out later, from neighbors, the night the lights went out, and from people waiting with me for the trolleybus that never came. How they fled with their bundles of eiderdowns, Virgin Marys, and cut-crystal glasses when the Sudetenland was annexed. And how they came back from the Protectorate, illegally, without a pass, creeping around fences in the dark and calling in calming whispers to their dogs, who weren't deported, to smuggle in chrysanthemums on All Saints' Day.

THEN WAR BROKE OUT. On the stripped plain between Most and Litvínov, near the village of Záluží, construction got under way on a giant factory complex for the production of synthetic fuel: Hydra-Werke — the Hydra. An indestructible monster. The Germans brought in some hundred and fifty thousand POWs and forced laborers, set up concentration camps, and began to build a road. They clear-cut the forests and the boars fled into the mountains. Prisoners were buried where they fell. Anywhere a bulldozer excavates ground for a new site around here, it plows human bones.

In the space of two years, a chemical plant sprang up on the quaking bogs where once there had been millions of frogs, and a housing complex for the workers and engineers took root amid the fresh-cut clearing. Machines, roads, railroads, flats with bathrooms and central heating. The complex was conceived by a top German architect with a feel for urban design and the horror of the times. Meanwhile the prisoners trampled down all the vegetation to bare rock and a decaying core of lignite. The factory began operation, and ever since, its smokestacks have been sprinkling the landscape for miles in every direction with a fine, almost imperceptible, layer of caustic ash.

The birds have long since moved away, and children stand dumbstruck over the occasional dead butterfly blown in by the wind. Sunups here are gray, hazy, and bleak, the only sound the roar and whistle of trains in the distance and the dull thud of the factory that runs three shifts around the clock.

Early in the war, squadrons of American bombers overflew the plant, paying it no attention. People would come running out of the halls and workshops and turn their faces to the filtered sun, listening to the engines' drone as they tracked the silvery dots' progress across the gray-blue sky. Then one day, as they were changing shifts, the bombs began to fall. Hydrogen sulfide leaked from shattered tubing, cisterns burned and distillation towers toppled. The dead, who perished in the inadequate shelters, were covered over the next day with a combination of rubble and earth, and the rebuilding of the monstrous chemical facilities began atop the ruins, a frenzied tangle of assemblages and conduits, almost as if to represent the dying's final spasms.

After that, people fled at the first sound of the alarm, bowling over fences, hanging off the sides of trucks and falling beneath the wheels, fighting over bicycles, zigzagging across the fields pursued by low-flying fighter jets with empty window frames held over their heads, or crawling under old, half-rotten potato baskets. Mothers from the surrounding villages went to work the nearby mines before daybreak, children in their arms, pushing newborns in carriages, descending into the shafts with no headlamps, ten to a cage. I know a man who saw with his own eyes a mother in Růžodol, still drowsy after working the night shift, run out of her burning home and forget her child inside. She went back and dragged away the burning beams with her bare hands, while a young man from the mountains, seized with temporary insanity, sat on the road with a violin in a rain of grenade shrapnel, between detonations playing "Bohemia the Beautiful, Bohemia of Mine." There were seventeen of those air raids before the war was through, and close to a hundred thousand people died in them.

To this day, the bare, trampled plain around the factory remains pockmarked with craters, which pool up with water when it rains. Children fish plankton out of them for the goldfish in their aquariums, and every now and then they dredge up an unexploded bomb.

After the war, the Hydra was rechristened the Stalin Works and the POWs from all over Europe, assuming they had survived, returned home. The concentration camps were converted into barracks for the volunteer work brigades by removing the barbed wire and hanging a board over the gate with the words STALINITES' HOME. It was in one of these barracks that Joska the miner slept with a knife under his pillow, and in another that Sviták mauled the Pomykal family. That came later, though. First they had to recruit Czechs to resettle the borderlands. People flocked here from all over the country to take the place of the Germans expelled after the war — "gold diggers," for the most part, who soon moved back to the interior, but there are also still those who on New Year's drink toasts out of glasses from the Chevra Kadisha burial society, plundered from the Germans, who stole them from the Jews, and attend commemorations of the Great October Revolution in second- and third-hand lambskin coats, acquired in the same way; young people who hoped to build a new life here; Slovaks and gypsies from Prešov and Snina, many of whom had never traveled by train before they came here; repatriates from the Franco-Belgian coal basin; the idealists, eager to "boost the economy," and the luckless, assigned here against their will or come to forget their wartime losses; professors and doctors freshly minted with accelerated degrees, having waited seven years for them inside the Protectorate, at the Avia aircraft factory, or outside it, under the rain of bombs in Dortmund; young ladies sent here to teach for two years and now starting in on their second decade, passing their evenings like old maids, on creaky chairs bought for ten crowns from the National Renewal Fund.

Nevertheless, ignoring the warning signs of those who died in agony, buried under the distillation columns, and the ancient wisdom that there are places where the grass won't grow a hundred years, they decided to build a modern socialist urban center here, a city of the future. One group of architects drew up a set of tidy plans with scenes of children playing, which served as the basis for construction of a community of model homes, while another designed a collective house for fifteen hundred people — with a cinema, a café, a nursery school, day-care centers, shops, a hairdresser's, a lecture hall, and an electric refrigerator. The daily *Mladá fronta* ran photographs of the plans, reproduced so poorly that it shifted them into the realm of fiction, alongside poems by Vladimir Mayakovsky and Jiří Orten, all this in the days when we were marching in May Day parades, singing the song with the refrain "Lidice–Most–Litvínov."

Some of us went off to build this future metropolis. Again, trees were chopped down and lime corroded the vegetation. Campfires burned at construction sites on hot summer nights and young people sang songs of revolution, loyally alternating between "Chant des Partisans" and "It's a Long Way to Tipperary" or "White Army, Black Baron" and "John Brown's Body." And afterward, as the fire died, they walked off in couples into the unfinished homes with no roofs.

And I believe that here in this house, in this very room, where my bookshelf, bed, and desk now stand, where the door opens with a thud all by itself, a young man and a young woman one warm night sat on a mortar trough. I believe that they kissed here, underneath the stars, and spoke to each other in whispers about the future inhabitants of the homes they were building. I believe it because in those days nothing was lost yet, and also because it's an ancient theme, the endlessly reworked motif of the head of the family who plants a tree for his grandchildren, because it's a great and fundamental theme of the future, human solidarity, and hope.

And that was how it really was, in those first years after the war, when we ended even our love letters with the slogan *Honor to work!* We dreamed up our own destiny in a self-destructive messianic dream of a workers' tomorrow. I believe that that young couple arranged my furniture in their minds, and with their kissing prefigured my own kisses to come. I believe that that young woman, leaning out the window opening over an arid wasteland with a French prisoner of war's bleached bones jutting up from the soil, predicted your dread, my sweet, that once-in-a-lifetime morning by the riverside when dewdrops rolled down the rusty wire fence, that she predicted your nighttime tears, my darling Jakub, long before I ever met your mother.

Yes, my poetics are the poetics of a policeman; I gather facts: I'm not writing a story, but giving tes-

timony. And I say that it's true, that that's the way it was, I say it now, here, *midway upon the journey of our life*, quivering with the cold of the midnight wind that whipped around Dante's ears when he found himself standing alone amid the mist and darkness.

It was for our sake that these homes were built, because of our dread of the dark and the rain that those two Italian trolleybuses were purchased with precious hard currency, and for our safety that they erected yellow-and-black signs around the factory, warning DANGER, MINEFIELD!

II

FOR ONCE AGAIN THE FACTORY was encircled with barbed wire, and once again wooden watchtowers, perched atop four long legs, were erected around the perimeter. The factory guard was reinstated, and the sirens, abandoned and left to the elements in the first years after the war, were repaired and put back in service.

We were getting older. Long before our revolutionary dream became a reality, the concrete calendar of the road was overgrown with grass. The era of brigades and campfires had come to an end, and the gardens' stunted trees had been covered over in sickly leaves more than once. In the early fifties, as fighting broke out around the thirty-second parallel — that is, shortly after Záviš Kalandra died with a noose around his neck and the poet Josef Palivec was condemned, because he knew that the darkness cherishes amber, darkness of burrows, darkness omnivorous, that is, when a huge barn for sorting books was erected on Na Maninách Street in

Prague, with a team of musclemen hired to tear apart the spines of works by Pascal and Thomas Aquinas, and the fairy tales of Božena Němcová illustrated by Artuš Scheiner, and the writings of Masaryk and Deml and Ladislav Klíma, and illuminated medieval missals, and, as they came rolling in off the conveyor belt, Vasari and Lessing, and of course Olesha and Bunin and Merezh-kovsky and Babel — the concrete road finally reached the Collective House. Atop the edifice, a little spruce adorned with colorful ribbons fluttered gaily in the wind.

The gypsies found out they were eligible for a ration of low-priced coke from the factory, stopped tearing up the floorboards for heat, and formed a folk music group to showcase the rich tradition of popular culture. They had a cimbalom shipped in from Slovakia, and began playing at the Collective House's newly opened café. Saturdays and Sundays they would perform until past midnight, and on payday the foremen and technicians from the Stalin Works would plaster ten-crown notes to the musicians' sweaty foreheads in accordance with the old custom.

Then one day, at long last, the Collective House filled with people. Balconies were draped with laundry to dry, children ran the hallways playing spy and kick-ing balls, and the odor of exhaust from the ventilated kitchens hung over the landings, blending together into an aroma of well-being. Some amenities, however, turned out to be unusable, and the new era, bringing new needs the planners hadn't foreseen, required further modification. Residents stopped using the shared fridge when they realized food was being stolen, lockers for grocery deliveries ended up storing old shoes, and the projected library turned out to be a police station instead. The lecture hall plays host to a magic show every now and then, or doctors fielding questions from a few older women worried about cancer.

Most of the elderly, though, are dying off. Their hearts can't take the climb to the ninth or eleventh floor when the elevators are out of order. The very first spring an old engineer died on the landing between four and five, and shortly after, they also took away his wife with a heart attack, a fatal act of class justice, since a childless couple like them hardly needed such a spacious flat. Also on some days there is no water. That's life for you. People take pitchers and watering cans to fill them from a spring in the woods, which, alas, is drying up. There were times when there was no heat, and the freezing men and women coming home at the end of a shift had no choice but to climb right into bed.

Only on Saturday, after payday, you could get quietly drunk on rum. That was how babies were made. Swing shift.

CHILDREN WERE BEATEN from an early age and raised on the story of little Pavlik Morozov, without any great success. And they grew up. Every now and then, a boy would drown in one of the flooded pits behind the Collective House, or a girl would be raped by a gang of pimply apprentices — but statistically it was negligible. So they grew up and the Party and the government decided to build a city of young people, an apprentices' boarding school, in a valley in the mountains above Litvínov, on land registered to the village of Schönbach.

And again, for the God knows how manyth time, the trees were chopped down and some twenty sad gray buildings, with all the most modern conveniences, rose up out of the plowed mud of a construction site. Now the trade school blocks stand shoulder to shoulder, in tight formation, glowering over the soft curve of the woods.

The school's management purchased several hundred portraits of statesmen, equipment for piping radio broadcasts directly into the dormitories, beds, wardrobes, chairs, sinks, chess sets, and volleyballs.

Then, in September, the fathers, sweating profusely, delivered their children to school. They sat through welcoming speeches by the deputy minister and the school's director, toured the new facilities with nods of appreciation, and sang the "Song of Work" before heading back to Litvínov, where, having fulfilled their responsibility and relieved to have one less mouth to feed at home, they knocked back a few pints and succumbed to the impulse to open up about their years in the army. Meanwhile, in the school canteen, which still smelled of glue and plaster, the boys, heckling the girls squealing at the next table, devoured a meal of fried cutlets and Russian salad before being marched back to the dormitories, where every enrollee was issued a regulation uniform.

It was an occasion for much rejoicing, filled with pranks and merriment, according to one prominent Czech writer, who reported that even the culturally backward gypsy Petrášek, in her words, "enchanted with his newly acquired possessions, laid his miner's apprentice wardrobe across the bedroom's four lower bunks and, alone in his boxers, caressed the neatly folded work clothes and the rubber boots that go with it, the sweat suit for home wear, the everyday uniform with pilot's cap, the dress uniform of dark cloth with epaulets, the military-style cap braided with miner's insignia, the wool overcoat, rain jacket, gym shoes, socks, and dress shirt and tie to go with the uniform."

We often read stories like that in the papers, and we often saw boys and girls in the weekly newsreel eating

from plates piled with hearty fare or, dressed in their sweat suits, playing volleyball and chess. That was still in the dark years around 1950, when we stood anxiously over a map of the world, in that time of stifling summer evenings on a boarded-up Wenceslas Square, when Alice, leaning against the Darex display window, wept quietly with longing for Paris.

Meanwhile the boys found a second home in the trade school. They too settled in. Evenings were devoted to self-help, as they took in the pant legs on their dark dress uniforms and widened the cuffs with the remnants, removed the filling from the shoulder pads in their uniform jackets, dipped their hair in sugar water and curled it back from their low foreheads with a cooking spoon, because along with Lucia Bosè, Jean Marais had also reappeared on movie screens.

They told them over and over, day after day, that they were the youth of the world, the revolutionary avant-garde of the working class. But the world was arranged perfectly now, people were living better and better every year, and there were no more mysteries to be revealed. The revolution covered up her nakedness and got fat, spending her evenings staring at the TV screen. Suddenly it turned out there was no motivation. No perspective. We were caught in a trap.

Truth and lies weren't antinomies, but dialectical opposites. Every reality — according to the bitter teachings of Shklovsky, who wasn't concerned with the state of the cotton market but only with methods of weaving — every thing can be named with any word, and every word can mean any thing. Even joy. Even hope. Even love. So young people tenaciously applied themselves to tables and chairs, sinks, door handles, electrical wiring. On long winter nights they threw their penknives at the door paneling, braided insulation tubing from loudspeakers into horseshoes to bring themselves luck, tore up the tiles in the bathroom, broke the windows, and shot out the lightbulbs with air rifles from the Svazarm paramilitary. Having set to work dismantling the gray-and-white structures stone by stone, they declared a war, vicious and renewed every year, against their instructors, lazy, fearful, and embittered men, who either gave up eventually or took to drink.

"Just go ahead and kick me out," the trainees say defiantly. "Go ahead, I don't care. I'm a miner and who can say more!"

I cross paths with them, dull-eyed and silent, Sunday morning on the deserted main road. Masturbated white, they banter with the women from the local textile plant, drinking beer at the tap or leaning their backs against a wall, watching lethargically as a half-empty tram crawls along the sunbaked street. Sprawled across the decayed stairs in front of the closed door of a church, or swaggering suggestively in front of the record store window.

"Man oh man, that is hoppin'! Pa-pa-papidda-pa. . ."

"No, no, no, no! There won't be any war!" R. A. Dvorský declares in a jazzy rhythm.

They all have painted neckties, gaudy symbols of virility that they wear with the timidity and fierce defiance of exhibitionists. The authorities waged a long campaign against the ties, to no avail. You are manifesting sympathies for the capitalist West, the young men were told. You are flirting with imperialism, comrades. But they were not, and in most cases they recognized that it was unacceptable for a member of the Communist Youth to walk the streets of a traditional mining town with a picture of a cowboy on their chest. So they bought their ties at the annual fair, painted with patriotic motifs: the equestrian statue of St. Wenceslas in the middle, Prague Castle at the bottom, and the Powder Tower on the knot; a village out of a painting by Mikoláš Aleš, a herd of cows, and a pine tree on the knot; a busty female Spartakiad gymnast, Strahov stadium, and a pair of crossed maces; Tatraplan, Tudor, Sedan, the pride of the nation's automotive industry; a cinder track, Zátopek, spiked shoes; Moscow University, bottom to top. I haven't seen a tie with a portrait of Julius Fučík or the Party symbol. But the young man dancing a jerky tango in front of the loudspeaker on the street this desperate, desolate Sunday morning has a tie with a faithful portrait of the Kremlin and Red Square with Lenin's mausoleum.

"If I had me a little canoe, over the river and far away," he says.

"My Moscow, my country. . ." the Russian words resound across the empty square, echoing up to the church bells, baked white in the noonday sun. The salesgirl gets a bonus for playing Soviet songs.

"Man oh man, a dog at least!" says the second of the bunch. "I'd train him to follow me around. And jump over things."

"Pa-pa-papee-da, pa-pa-dee-da," says the third. And they all agree: "What a drag, man, what a drag!"

"Death," says Dante, "death could scarce be more bitter than that place."

They walk away, the one in front stuffing his flashy tie between his coat lapels, so that Lenin's mausoleum is hidden and only the onion towers of Saint Basil's Cathedral are poking out of his neckline. Yes, *this* is the future. It will be like this everywhere. I'm writing about our town in the sixth decade of the twentieth century. I'm writing about the future. One day it will be like this everywhere, this is the future. Athematic prose. But make no mistake: Here, one day, all the joy in the world must blossom forth, because there is no way to live sustainably without joy and hope. "But since it came to good, I will recount all that I found there revealed by God's grace."

HERE THERE IS EVERYTHING. But it is not the encounter between an umbrella and a sewing machine on an operating table, the miraculous certainty that a butterfly will take flight at the point where my line of sight intersects yours, my beloved, if I think of you, the certainty that you will come, that someday, if I long for it badly, you will come again, striding across the stony wasteland underneath my window, between the nursery school and the crèche, fair-haired and seventeen, with a red-and-white range pole in hand. Alas, I'm not telling my stories to make sense of the absurd. No crazy tram operator is suddenly going to veer off and drive us through the meadows and ponds with gulls flashing white against the blue backdrop of sky, because the cast-iron wheel with the handle isn't a steering wheel but a brake.

Here there is everything. Absolutely and without restriction. Language in its lexical state, where every reality is potentially confronted with the entire framework of discourse.

You little slut! say the mothers cuddling with their children at the entrance to the children's clinic, and my neighbor, if he wants to say of a woman that she's more beautiful than beautiful, calls her typical.

"You doing all right?" I ask him as we walk to the trolleybus together and the silence gets too much to take.

"Oh, you know, same old same old."

"You on morning crew?"

"Yep. Long as I'm pullin' down eighteen, that's what it's all about. Eighteen hunnerd's the living wage. Sixteen to the wife, two in the pocket. Plus bonuses too, it's understood. Still, she's gotta hustle, gotta make do, put that meat on the table at night. Yep, times were," he says, turning melancholy, "times were you could make some real dough. Back when I was runnin' the convoy from Slovakia to Hungary, truck commander for the UNRRA, yep. We had these berets like the English army and uniforms without any rank. Everyone called us captain at least. That's right, and I'll tell you, when we'd run dry, I'd be, hey, boys, let's load one up for ourselves! One time we got a whole tankful of white wine, young stuff, still bitter. We sold it to the café owners in Budapest. Ever been?"

"No."

"You should see it. Like Prague, only world-class. But they got a Castle and Vyšehrad there, too. Yep, so we parked the truck, and Richard, this fella from Ostrava, he pumped that vino like gasoline. Could've swum in it, we had so much. And that's what we did, man. Those girls there, Hungarians, know what I mean? They got sloshed soon as they climbed in, like it soaked through their skin or somethin'. I could tell you stories, but truth is, that's not my thing. I'm more of a moralist. Watchin', though, that's all right. Listen in on the action. We had some laughs, I'm tellin' you. Had some real good laughs."

By now I know all his stories by heart. This is one of his five recurring themes. If the trolleybus is running late, he tells me again how they sold sacks of coffee filled two-thirds with peas, or else I get to hear a well-intentioned sentimental novella about three foreigners, that is, him and "his three boys," who saved a sick and suffering girl from death by starvation, and the mistress of one of the officers, who would always wait for the convoy in the middle of the bridge over the Danube.

"The Danube," he says, "now that's a river. Too wide even to swim across. I kid you not!"

"It's not coming," I say.

"Yep, times were," he goes on, "back before the war! I remember when bein' a technician meant you were somebody. That's what they always told us at Škoda: Boys, being a technician is a great honor. And a responsibility. A technician's got to maintain himself. Not like those greasy coveralls they all wear nowadays. I was just a greenhorn fresh off my apprenticeship and I kept myself spick and span. When the boss called you in, you gave your hands a good washing and put on a jacket. And a necktie, buddy. Without a tie he wouldn't even talk to you."

Now he starts to expand on one of his favorite themes. The story-cum-myth about the elegant boss who smilingly gestures to the chair: "Have a seat, friend!" He doesn't sit, he remains standing up, he knows his etiquette.

"Mr. Chief Foreman, sir," he says solemnly, clicking his heels so smartly it sends up a spray from the thin layer of mud coating the ground at the trolleybus stop. "Foreman Antonín Steklý reporting. And the boss stands up, shakes my hand, and says: We've got a job for you. Special order. To a thousandth of an inch. You need people? So I give it a look and say: We can do it, sir. I'll need four men. Take five, he says. And I left. And we did it. Course nowadays, we have some laughs."

"Here it comes," I say. As we move slowly forward in the line for the bus, he pulls something out of his pocket and shoves his big calloused hand in my face.

"Look!"

"What is it?"

"It's a medal. What are you, blind?"

"Mm, nice."

"Right? It's from the Sokol race."

"You ran that?"

"Do I look like an idiot?"

"How'd you lay your hands on it?"

"Someone gave it to me. It's a beaut."

"Oh," I say as we're torn apart by the stream of people pouring onto the packed vehicle. "Be good now!"

"See you!" he shouts at me over the heads of the crowd, and elbowing a space for himself he pins on his new medal next to the Party insignia, the badge of the North Bohemian Brown Coal District, and his two sapper's hammers.

Nearly all the men wear some kind of badge or insignia. Crossed hammers, athletic club badges, commemorative medals — visible signs of fitting in, amulets against the creeping fear. And they're easy to come by: They sell them at every local fair and park of culture and recreation.

Under certain conditions, life puts up almost no resistance. Matter is infinitely pliant, it's the triumph of technology over raw material, *die Welt als Wille und Vorstellung*. The world of men. The dimensions of human architecture were strictly limited by the height of the tallest trees — and as we know, no tree grows to heaven. A monograph was an unthinkable luxury prior to the invention of the letterpress. Gothic architecture is, in the final analysis, always a struggle in vain with material. With nature as a feminine principle.

But you don't even have to attend a vocational school for miners to realize that *Werther* is a hodge-podge of styles. And I didn't kill myself either, my dear, though it would have made for a nice funeral amid the perfume of those heroic lilacs, though it would have been such an easy way to attain my potential. But in fact there was no reason to kill oneself. Except perhaps for a lack of potential, because in those days life put up scarcely any resistance and revolution glittered at the point of the Red Army's bayonets. It was a great triumph of mind over matter.

Only a sense of modesty kept them from adding a fourteenth, fifteenth, and eighteenth floor to the Collective House, only their joy at possessing a hidden strength kept them from raising a granite head of Stalin in the thin air of our mountains. For here, truly, there is everything.

The American tie with a picture of Lenin's tomb on it, the STALINITES' HOME sign over the gate of camp 17/18, the Plexiglas Venus de Milo, James Joyce in a blue cloth binding in the window of a used bookstore in Most on a stifling rainy day in the mid nineteen fifties, Alice on the embankment in a nylon petticoat with the panorama of Prague Castle behind her, paying fifty hellers to look at sunspots, the illegible carbon copy of the prophecy of a young blind man, the one-armed accordionist on the steam train running the Litvínov–Chomutov line, the muzzled poet in a white tuxedo, saxophone in hand, doubled over in pain from a chronic inflammation of the small intestine, the film by Marcel Carné that costs an extra crown admission, the last of the Greats in a greenish Russian tunic tearing up over Boris Pasternak's *Blank Verses*, and Pasternak himself in an unheated shack leaking rain, the encyclical *Rerum novarum* and the poet whose verses the children of the tired policeman fold into paper airplanes, the trees and the nettles that still remained here, and the washerwomen by the river, and the water and the unfinished beer and you, you, shivering and in pain, coming to ask me to remain faithful to you, and everything . . . and everything . . . and everything . . .

THERE IS NO WAY TO MAKE SENSE of nonsense. And this is an entirely ordinary, everyday encounter between an umbrella and a sewing machine on an operating table, because the Fashion Design production collective is moving into the surgical ward and it's raining.

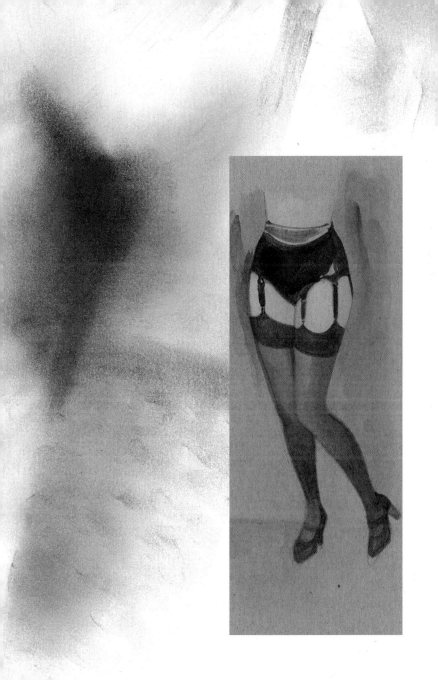

And here comes an elderly man with a woman, walking through the mud. She is pale with exhaustion and pain, leaning on him for support. His left eyelid is wounded, making it look as though he were winking.

"So what seems to be the matter?" the young doctor asks.

"He beat me, doctor. He kicked me, like I wasn't even a woman."

"Kicked you? Who?"

"Him, this one here," the woman bursts out sobbing. The man stands silently, clutching a scuffed black lady's handbag in his hand.

"He kicked you?" the doctor says.

"In the stomach!" the woman replies through her tears.

The man peers at the doctor through his half-shut eye, as if trying to give some sort of secret signal laden with meaning, but it's just that he can't control his injured eyelid. Unintentionally, he's exploiting the mishap to his advantage. Outside, the rain falls ceaselessly on the umbrella and the sewing machine on the operating table.

"Would you come with me, ma'am?" says the doctor. "Not you, you wait here!"

In the room next door, the doctor palpates the woman's abdomen and, apart from a few bruises, finds no serious injury.

"Put your clothes on," he says, then asks: "Is that your husband?"

"Who, him? No!"

"Then who is he?"

"I can't tell you."

"But you say he was kicking you in the stomach?"

"Yes. Would you be so kind as to make me out a certificate to that effect?"

"I can't do that if I don't know who you are," the doctor says, opening the door for the woman.

"I know," the woman says, "and you're going to call the police."

"May I ask you one small question?" the man interjects with a knowing smile, standing in front of the door still holding the handbag.

"Be my guest."

"What's wrong with the lady?"

"You should know better than me, don't you think?"

"I'm not the doctor here," says the man.

"Beat it!" the doctor yells.

"All right, but one more question."

"What?"

"Is it serious?"

"No. Good-bye!"

"Thank you, thank you kindly," the man says, handing the woman her bag so he can offer his arm again.

They walk away — they walk away, forever unfathomable, into the thickening darkness. The young doctor lights a cigarette, lies down on the sofa, and by memory, eyes closed, switches on the radio behind his head. Slowly a woman's alto emerges out of the unbounded space of night, anonymous as the angel on the right-hand side who swallowed the book with seven seals: ". . . *Klavierkonzert in D-moll, Köchel-Verzeichnis Nr. 466, von Wolfgang Amadeus Mozart.*" The door opened by itself. Now the pause in which a girl takes off all her clothes while gunfire explodes outside, followed by a moment of silence, and then the song begins.

First, a tragic minor chord from the strings, accented with intermittent blows on the timpani. A landscape, desolate and gutted, with the dissonant motifs of smokestacks on cello. Everything. Everything. Along the road a car approaches, rain murmuring in its headlights. In the opposite direction, advancing in staggering slow motion, two hunched figures pull a four-wheeled wagon. Now the complex tonal architecture unexpectedly gives way to the primal melody of the sweetly rippling countryside. Electrical wires and telephone cables, in the long, rounded tones of flutes and oboes, trace the land's outline, blurred by string glissandos of smoke and fog. Over and over again, it repeats. Willing puddles, unquenchable and in vain, reflect the stars. A steam shovel's brass headlights. Suddenly it's apparent that the meaning of that tragic opening chord is neither darkness nor the slow-motion stagger of the man and woman with the wagon, but, ascending by half steps, the material of the dark, dank buildings inside the gate that says STALINITES' HOME. Laid bare, the primal motif hugs the landscape's gentle contours. The puddles gape open in vain, like general pauses. And then it all condenses into an anguished, chaotic cacophony, narrowly rescued by the collective human pulse of the tympani.

AND I, LEANING OUT THE WINDOW, greedily inhale the odor of hydrogen sulfide. The fragrance of the hair of the unattractive women on the night trolleybuses, the fragrance, crushing as a pleasure denied, of the Tesla factory hall in Strašnice that cruel winter of '49.

They assigned me, bewildered, an intruder against my will, a locker with a young toolmaker. It was plastered with Man Ray nudes, which confirmed me in my belief that the revolution had been betrayed. It was a few days before Christmas, so the first thing I did was get my ration of Christmas Eve carp, which back then

they reserved for the working class. It was cold and I had no warm clothing, underwear, or gloves. At first I wore an old gray pair of pigskin gloves that my father had brought back from Paris when he was still alive. The galvanized sheets in the sheet-metal shop bristled with frost, and carols played from the loudspeakers during breaks.

A fat foreman named M. suffered a stroke at his workbench early one morning around Christmas. They took him away on a forklift, while the in-house radio station broadcast Chopin's funeral march throughout the factory. I cried that day, hidden behind a shelf of rolled alloy steel, for I was just a boy, still far from knowing that it would be my destiny to testify to these deaths. The dark and disharmonic material of the night pulses with the timpani's rhythm. I lean out the window, resembling absolutely nothing, exactly halfway between the constellation of Aldebaran and the gold tooth of a drunkard lying unconscious with his mouth open on the doorstep of his locked house. And all of a sudden the epic cadence of a piano intrudes upon the scene. Mitja Nikisch is getting down to business. The punch clocks ding. End of shift. And I'm still here, softly saying what is and what will be. Motivating the athematic syuzhet. I am seeking the motivation for my fate.

IT SEEMS SIMPLE ENOUGH: I was born the year Lindbergh made his first flight across the Atlantic, the year the protest march on Red Square by Lev Davidovich was dispersed with galoshes. In Göttingen electrons were still peacefully orbiting the nucleus, and it wasn't yet certain what color your eyes would be, as the constellation of your birth was still in preparation. My parents taught me to walk in Strakonice, on a beige blanket with a meander border, the same November evening the New York Stock Exchange collapsed. We still listened to the wireless on headphones in those days, and evenings were short. The only sound to be heard in the long hours till we fell asleep were the monotonous études for contrabass from the window across the way, played by a member of the Czech Philharmonic. There was tuberculosis, cancer, heart disease, and alcoholism in the family.

Then, around the time when the whale skeleton and the ostrich egg at the museum both fell under the same category of big to me, the Japanese invaded Manchuria. I learned to read from my mother's cookbooks, and one of the first words I could sound out was *Hitler*. Also *Baťa* and *Stalin*. At school they taught me using the Global Method; supposedly it was for bright children. Generally speaking, I was a bright child, and the foundation of my education in those days was built on my reading of a magazine called *The Little Reader*. Without which to this day I still wouldn't know that the bullet cast for me under strict specifications bears the beautiful name Atropos. I yearned to own a marionette puppet stage, and prayed for one in secret. And I used to imagine I had an underground cabin, warm and cozy and filled with children's furniture, where I could play with the little girl from across the street.

It seems simple enough, then, to find a motivation. On questionnaires about my political background, I usually state that I'm from a petty bourgeois family, but that even as a child I felt ashamed when I saw the poverty of proletariat children in Žižkov. Which is, at bottom, true. In the context of the biographical prose of political questionnaires, it is for that matter a canonical motivation, and, as such, the only possible one. It is politically incorrect for someone to try to conceal this fact: My childhood girlfriend, a lawyer, the daughter of a big Prague divorce attorney, usually states that she comes from the large family of an intellectual worker and that they have always lived in a rented flat and never owned their home. This too works, in its own way, although violating the principle that Shklovsky designates by the term *prijom*.

Hers is an eminently utilitarian application of the theme of *Prince Bajaja*, also known as *The Swineherd*.

It's the ancient theme of Ulysses returning to Ithaca dressed as a beggar. But strictly speaking, it's impossible, for there is no hope: For the motif of muteness and sheepskin, the motif of beggarly filth and the infirmity of old age, never find resolution in a moment where the golden locks are let down in all their glory and Ulysses the Cunning takes up the great bow and bends it with ease. My childhood girlfriend often goes to the café with Alice, without any messenger from Darex ever appearing at Alice's door bearing gifts of fancy lingerie and a twinset of gasoline-green woolen sweaters.

Antti Aarne identified — apparently once and for all — roughly seven hundred themes to which all folktales can be reduced. These themes appear in various incarnations, however, rarely in their original form, and are typically decanonized. Thus the canonical theme of shelter, a roof over one's head, is the Parthenon (sky-blue against the blue of the sky!), a perfect albeit noncanonical realization of family happiness: polished living room, washing machine, refrigerator, and healthy children.

Yet decanonization usually happens in solitude, on an individual basis. Its symptoms are suffering and bitterness.

My theme, if I may say such a thing nowadays, here, in this windy room, with the neighbor whistling a hackneyed wartime hit beneath my window, is the decanonized theme of the journey and faithfulness. Actually, the two are connected: the impulse to journey can be continually restored only through faithfulness. But the depressing thing is that *this* theme has no universal canonization *at all*, it motivates itself and can be realized only as fate. Only by being realized and finished once and for all does it make, or not make, sense. And it is this theme, therefore, that is absolutely forbidden in the context of one's political profile.

Because in this situation, faced with the hunchbacked and impeccably dressed personnel officer, with his pipe and open-necked Youth Union shirt, one cannot say with Diderot: "What business is it of yours? If I start delving into interpretations of the purpose for the journey, then it's farewell, Jacques's love!" And yet that's what I'm saying, that's exactly what I'm saying, my dear, past and future, passing by, yes, I'm saying *farewell!* Farewell, my love! Because the only thing that matters here is the interpretation of the purpose for the journey.

I WAS SIXTEEN the year of the Battle of Stalingrad. My wife spent the winter in Terezín while we were preparing to take our first dance classes. It is, it seems, a grand and glorious thing. I know a lady who, at the birth of her second child, burst into tears on learning

Světozor

that it was another boy: "Well, that's that. I'm never going to have a daughter I can bring to dance class!"

My classmates had black suits made. Fabric was hard to come by in those years, but there were some who had their own supply — for instance, a friend of mine whose father was a bank manager and whose family owned plantations in Madagascar. He and a few of the other boys had tuxes. One of the girls had a white gown sewn at Podolská's. That winter, I was told, most of the Jewish girls in Terezín stopped having their periods.

Around then was the first time I read the *ABC of Dialectical and Historical Materialism*, by Antar, who was a physician and among whose many achievements was the decision of my wife's roommate to leave the monastic order so that, through diligent study of Russian and shorthand, she could work her way up to head of the Revolutionary Trade Union Movement. The scar of her sweet blasphemy, as she removed the veil at the beginning of her last night of virginal innocence, remained inside all of us forever. "Deep," my friend, "deep are the claws of communism sunk into us!"

We had tended to look down on the girl before February, since she was from Haná, in the Moravian countryside, and every week she would receive a package of pastries, bacon, and black sausage from home. So it is that everything is connected and we become the contents of our own story. Of course we ate the sausages with her, purely out of loyalty, and besides, money was low. But still, to this day, whenever I descend to the ground floor of our model home to make myself coffee, pressing myself to the wall to avoid being seen by my vigilant neighbors, I watch the pot uneasily as the water gurgles and churns, the surface roiling and rippling in a process I learned to view as a revolutionary transition from quantity into quality. Also the toilets sometimes stink of uric acid, which as everyone knows, can now be produced synthetically, thanks to advances in science and technology.

These were classic examples of verification of theory by praxis. Examples of the knowability of the world. I believe that the world is knowable, I believe that art is a combination of labor and construction and method, though I never did find out what alizarin dye was. Actually, I didn't even want to find out, since I was utterly content to imagine it as a shade of grayish blue, the color of pigeons, ash, the color of your dress, my dear, the afternoon of my eighteenth birthday. "You of course don't remember what color dress you were wearing that day, but I do . . ." And the white lace sailor collar, halfway down the back, that heroic collar of the revolution and that handful of stubborn fools, dispersed with galoshes on Red Square the year that I was born.

DURING THE LAST YEARS OF THE WAR, half the subjects at school were taught in German, that is, in the broken and deliberately mangled German our professors were required to learn as part of their training. Besides, it wasn't totally useless: We read Rilke and Hölderlin and Georg Trakl and Johann Christian Günther, and also E.T.A. Hoffmann, long before we had any idea that he would become the spiritual godfather of not only our rational optimism but also our disillusion. We often skipped class to hang around the cinemas on the outskirts where they offered morning screenings for German army men. Scrawny girls stood around in front of the display cases filled with photographs of Zarah Leander and Marika Rökk, and I felt sorry for them, because back then I still thought it hurt when a girl's breasts grew in. We often didn't come home until after dark, through black streets humming with flashlights powered by manual generators. That last winter, I was invited several times to afternoon tea parties at the homes of my classmates. Most of the nightclubs were closed and the theaters weren't performing, but the girls were growing up nevertheless and needed to be taught manners. The tea, brewed from rosehips, was served with oat cakes on Meissen porcelain. They tasted of cold margarine, artificial honey, and mouse droppings. We listened to old Armstrong records with the volume turned down, and sometimes we would roll back the carpet so we could dance. Toward evening the master of the house, returning home from the office, would poke his head in the door and say:

"Is everyone having fun? Please, pardon me, I don't mean to interrupt. If I could just have a little quiet for fifteen minutes?"

We all knew that meant he was going to tune in to London in the room next door. Only trusted friends were invited, although the caution was a bit overdone, since on the map hidden under the rug in the gentlemen's parlor, the front line was always drawn circumspectly in accordance with the official reports of the German High Command.

That was our cue, then, to turn off the gramophone, eat cakes, and discuss the situation. In an odd way it was exciting, as now there was fighting going on in areas indicated on our school map of the Reich. And sometimes, when we would turn out the lights and open the windows after it rained, we could hear the muffled fire of artillery in the distance. Many of us were learning Cyrillic in secret.

One day I told one of my classmates, a girl who wore braids even though she was already putting on lipstick outside of school, that in Russia people weren't prejudiced, the relationship between a man and a woman was solely a matter of free choice, and the family played a minor role in the life of young people there — to no avail, of course, as everyone was always on their best behavior at our parties and, besides, the girl's father was the owner of a large design firm. To this day, I still remember her name, as her father's views on the high ethical function of socialist architecture appeared regularly in the press. Although she was a willing listener and even seemed to agree with me, alas, I never even touched her hand with the sharp, manicured nails.

Meanwhile the head of the house, invigorated by the encouraging words of Sir Bruce Lockhart, walked across the room and came to a stop behind our backs. Inspired by the girl's beauty, I was expounding at length. Finally, he intervened:

"You're naïve, son. You don't know what you're asking for. If we're occupied by the Russian army, that means bolshevism."

That was what I assumed. I didn't see his point. The girl suddenly burst into peals of laughter. Gesturing grandly with his shapely lawyer's hand, he added:

"None of you children has the slightest idea what bolshevism is."

"If it gets its clutches on you, you're dead," I replied, quoting the slogan from the poster plastered on every street corner in Prague. The old man blanched and walked out without a word. I was elated, because young women, as everyone knows, adore audacity and heroism.

Obviously, they never invited me back again, and years later they were still telling people that my wife and I were alcoholics and morphine addicts. Then the day came when the old man was assigned to the construction crew for the new bridge from Modřany to Chuchle. He labored on it until falling into the clutches of a rapidly progressive senile dementia, which prevented him from being transformed through contact with the working class and contributing to the building of brighter tomorrows.

I'VE BEEN TOLD THAT HE'S RETIRED now and suffers fierce insomnia. His eleven-year-old son beats him at chess every time, even when he sacrifices a rook. Most of his waking hours he spends sitting in his easy chair — him, the former bridge champion of Prague — playing solitaire.

"All right, Papa," his wife says, gingerly and tenderly, as night sets in. "Time for beddy-bye. Mr. Muk is here."

"Well then," the old man says, "send him on in! An ace is higher than a ten, isn't it?"

"Of course, Papa."

"I knew it!" says the old lawyer.

A short, bald, potbellied man in a black overcoat with a plush collar enters the living room. On the little finger of his left hand is an enormous antique ring with a chalcedony scarab.

"Good evening," the old man says, smiling. The bald man gives no reply, quietly passing through to the bedroom. The old man's son, reading a newspaper under a lamp, doesn't even lift his eyes, tugging unconsciously at the corner of his Pioneer scarf.

"Now, hurry up, Papa. We don't want to keep Mr. Muk waiting!" The old man's wife helps him to his feet, unbuttons his house coat, loosens his belt buckle, and guides him into the next room, following the bald man.

The lawyer stops in the doorway and, pants sagging around his waist, shouts back into the noiseless shadows: "Quiet!"

The boy goes on reading his newspaper. After a moment, the lady of the house emerges from the bedroom on tiptoe and carefully closes the door.

"Stop the clock, Pavel! I have to remind you every time!"

"Yes, right away!" says the boy. He laughs out loud at a joke in the paper.

"Sssh! Quiet! Can't you see that Mr. Muk is here?!"

She opens the grandfather clock herself and stops the pendulum. The time is eight thirty-two. She sits down by the lamp and asks in a whisper:

"Have you done your homework?"

"Yes."

"What was the assignment?"

"The mutiny on the *Potemkin*."

"And what did you learn?"

"Well, how first there were maggots in the meat, then the revolt, and finally a victory for working-class solidarity. What else, right?"

"Working-class solidarity?" says the lady, nestling the boy's head to her bosom. "You poor little thing!"

"Mommy, please, let go," says the boy, still absorbed in his reading.

The lady mechanically rakes up the cards on the table, squares them, and cuts the deck. Jack of clubs. "You're a good boy, Pavel. I'm glad you're making an effort," she says wearily, laying the card on the table face down.

Meanwhile, in the bedroom, the old man lies stretched out on one of the twin beds in a pair of dark-blue pajamas. Mr. Muk sits on a chair at the foot of the bed. "Close your eyes, close your eyes, close your eyes," the bald man in black repeats in a monotone.

The lawyer lies there, eyes closed, breathing heavily. Mr. Muk leans over and, reaching out his left hand adorned with the scarab ring, strokes the varicose veins protruding from the man's pale legs, all the while continuing his monotonous litany.

"Mama!" the old man suddenly cries out. "What is the *ut consecutivum* used for?"

"Shhh! You have to let go completely or I can't guarantee the result!" says Mr. Muk. "Please quietly recite the words along with me: *Pater noster, qui es in caelis, sanctificetur nomen Tuum, adveniat regnum Tuum . . .*"

Mr. Muk recites the words, his voice growing softer and softer, his eyelids sinking, until finally he falls silent. Air whistles softly in and out of his nose. The lawyer lies in bed, staring into the dark, while outside the trams ring like the bells for the elevation.

At ten thirty the old lady comes into the bedroom and wakes Mr. Muk. She has to, seeing as Mr. Muk, who puts people to sleep for a living, has fallen victim to an occupational hazard. He gets up and leaves as he came, silently, without a good-bye, exiting through the dark living room. The old lady lies down next to her husband and tries in vain to calm his muted tears. At last, exhausted, she falls asleep, while the lawyer lies awake till dawn, furiously searching his memory for the remains of his high-school knowledge. He dozes off just as the birds begin to chirp — at that sticky hour of morning when the overcrowded trolleybuses hurtle along the plain between Most and Litvínov, when the bells ding as the next shift punches in, at that insane and miraculous hour when I rise, filled with anxiety, the subject of your dream, my dear, at that hour of despair when God is silent, the devil is tired, and for once it is absolutely certain that the phone won't ring with some anxiously awaited piece of news.

SO OFTEN OUR FRAGILE HAPPINESS hangs on nothing more than the timid silence of old men.

An advertisement appeared in the local newspaper: "Selling lib. for fam. reasons. Techn., lit. & mus. Lot or indiv., view anytime, Hermína S." It gave an address in Most, fully spelled out. I stopped by late one afternoon. The house stood at the edge of a foul-smelling black gutter that I had been told was once a swift mountain stream crossed by stone bridges, with trout standing against the current underneath. I rang the bell at a door on the second floor with a brass plate announcing "Dr. Karel S., M.D.," and a label pasted on, instructing "ring 3x." A tousle-haired girl of about thirteen answered the door with her mouth full, and when I asked for Mrs. S, she just silently pointed to a wooden partition. From the half-open door behind her wafted the scent of crisply cooked meat, the pungent odor of boiled diapers, and a radio concert dedicated to the swing shift. I groped my way along the partition until suddenly a rep curtain pulled aside and I found myself face to face with a diminutive older lady. I introduced myself as a book collector and Mrs. S. ushered me into a room occupied by a set of glass-doored bookcases, a bed, and a two-burner gas stove on a countertop in the corner.

"If I may offer you a cup of tea," she said, "I can keep you company while you have a look around. The music scores are on the stand beneath the window. There wasn't any room left for the piano," she added in an apologetic tone.

The shelves were filled to overflowing, mostly with hulking volumes in three or four languages, a reminder of medicine's noble past, when it was still more a charitable consolation than a last recourse. None of them were museum pieces, let alone antiques, but putting up a front of incompetence I assembled a stack of about a dozen and a half nice editions on a small pedestal table with a lace doily.

"Sugar?" she asked, sitting down in a club chair across from me with a cup of light tea. "I'm delighted that you've found at least something to your taste. It would be a shame for it all to end up in the hands of a total stranger. I'm a widow, and I also lost my son in the war. It's all right," she said, fending off any gesture of sympathy. "Some people live longer than others, and they don't always go in the proper order. More tea?"

The two of us watched, fixated, as the thin stream of golden liquid filled the cups of fine porcelain webbed with tiny cracks. The strains of distant music and an infant's cries reached our ears from the other rooms in the flat, the black water flowed beneath the windows, and a fine coating of ash settled unceasingly onto the edges of those precious volumes, as it did onto the edges of my books back there, at the other end of town, an almost invisibly thin layer of gray-and-white, the fingerprints of loved ones long since buried underneath. Just then the telephone rang. Mrs. S. stood up, answered the call with her name, listened a moment, and then said in a kindly voice: "No, I'm sorry, no, really. Of course, it can happen to anyone. Good-bye!"

"Wrong number?" I asked.

"Yes, it always is. I don't have anyone left who would call. But people dial the wrong number more often than you might think. Making appointments, inquiring about train schedules, booking seats for the cinema. In fact, sometimes at night, when I can't sleep, I'll pick up the receiver and hear a voice coming through the static that reminds me of someone I used to know. The cheap folly of an old lady," she added with an embarrassed

smile. "But I don't mean to keep you. No, don't say a word. I enjoy talking. Truly I do."

The girl from next door stood on the staircase, with her mouth still full. I made my way home along the murky brook, the desolate landscape, furrowed with excavation, silhouetted by flares of waste gas.

Several times I was tempted to dial the number of Mrs. Hermína S., to arouse hope in her for one brief instant, to provide her a moment of great anticipation and delicious, heart-pounding excitement. Out of respect for the inexorableness of destiny, I never followed through.

Several times, late on one of those rainy evenings filled with hostile and unfathomable women, as I searched the felled trees for your fingerprints in vain, with everything catching me off guard and leaving me at a loss — several times now I had stepped into a phone booth, lifted the receiver, inserted a coin, and, after dialing the first two digits of the four-digit number that to my mind will forever represent the sum total of all the chasms of silence, hesitated while outside the trolleybuses and trams hurtled across the trampled plain and the watchtower lights blinked with dull regularity, until finally I was chased out in disgrace by the impatient pounding of someone with a matter that brooked no delay.

STILL, I THINK ABOUT THEM every day, the old lawyer and Mrs. S., at that hour of the morning when the alarm clocks ring and my child slides toward me under the covers and, two fingers in his mouth, closes his eyes in bliss.

He was born the year the first hydrogen bomb was tested, the year of the XIXth Congress of the CPSU, which is to say the year when shortly after we brought him home from the hospital, Grandfather Frost set out from the Chukotka Peninsula in Siberia in order to make it to Prague in time for Christmas Eve. Then he drove screeching through the city's muddy streets in a shabby sleigh from the National Theater's property storage room, while Snegurochka the snow maiden, with the bosom of a boyar, tossed flyers to the bewildered crowd. On one side they said, "Visit Grandfather Frost's Christmas market at the White Swan department store!" and on the other, under Picasso's dove, "Forward, people of goodwill, with Stalin and Klement Gottwald, for peace and socialism!"

When the day comes for my boy to write the canonical biographical prose of his political questionnaires, he will state that both his parents were intellectual workers and that his education exposed him to every layer of society, from nursery school on. He will probably learn a lot about atomic accelerators, but he isn't likely to learn that the eight-note whistle that he and the other children are playing beneath my window, manufactured from a material called Stalinite, is under certain social-historical conditions capable of making redheaded nymphs emerge naked from the forest thickets. He doesn't know, delight of my life, that he's marking time for the revolution on a syrinx. He doesn't know yet that I'm getting old. That I'm out of breath by the time I climb the stairs and step into the raw cold of this room whose door sometimes opens all on its own. He doesn't know I'm often thinking of death as we walk together hand in hand along the dug-up road with the foul-smelling mist hanging over it. He blows on his panpipes and, somewhere beyond the houses that the North Bohemian Brown Coal District built for its employees, the fauns timidly respond. The truncated crosses of TV antennas tower over the rooftops against the evening sky.

Thus did the first Christians draw the sign of a fish above their door, thus did they smear the door frames with lamb's blood in Egyptian times. Thus does everyone today subscribe to *Rudé právo*, so the destroying angel, the Angel of Death, passing along the mailboxes at dawn, will spare their firstborn child. And there are still other signs they post in the terrible struggle for life and death — white duvet covers, nylon lingerie, and, on Saturdays, upholstered chairs, bouquets of flowers and red flags, clothing themselves in the symbols of prosperity and cramming their children full of high-calorie food, so the little ones' sunken chests won't cast any doubt on their own conscientiousness and loyalty. On state-approved holidays they open the windows wide and sing at the top of their lungs, bolstering their good cheer with the feeling of a job well done.

I too got in the habit of walking around with a good-natured smile, even in the dark, since one can never be sure when one's portrait will suddenly be sliced out of the darkness in the beam of a pocket flashlight. I force myself to think of cheerful things as I lug my bulging briefcase up the steep hill alongside the cemetery, comforting myself that in the worst case I can blame the anxiety that comes over me every time I make the ascent on the difficulty I have breathing.

A high-tension pylon stands in the middle of the cemetery like a gigantic crucifix. The soil of the Litvínov cemetery is a poorly drained clay, and the coffins are lowered into a cloudy bath of yellowy brown. The lighter children's caskets float in the grave a moment before sinking beneath a layer of earth. The whole place is honeycombed with mine tunnels, and sometimes the ground shakes with underground explosions. Off in a corner sits the neoclassical tombstone of Pick the factory owner. The drunkards stop to piss on the back of it on their way home at night from the Cozy Corner pub, railing against their aging wives and their arthritis and the entire world as their classical urine eats away at the metal sheet intended to shield the stone from the elements. My child stands enthralled by the pattern of rusty spots, one of the rare irregularities in his life, then departs in silence, apparently still moved by the same emotion that drove tears to the eyes of Baudelaire's lover of passing clouds.

YET, IN SPITE OF IT ALL, here too the cemetery serves as a quiet refuge. And also, on sunny autumn days, when a man can bring himself to avow his dread for an instant amid the crackle of fallen leaves, a locus of shattered continuity: false of course, like everything about life here, since no matter how much he internalizes it, a stroll through tombstones engraved with strangers' names can be nothing more than a substitute gesture at best — and he tries in vain (like the time we lit candles on the abandoned tombs of soldiers at Olšany Cemetery in Prague) to enter into a time that is not his.

Almost every day at the cemetery you can run across an old man with a black briefcase who sits down on the edge of a tombstone, unwraps a thin sandwich with the crusts sliced off, and proceeds to eat, apportioning the crumbs equitably among the filthy sparrows gathered at his feet. This is Mr. A., the former coffin maker.

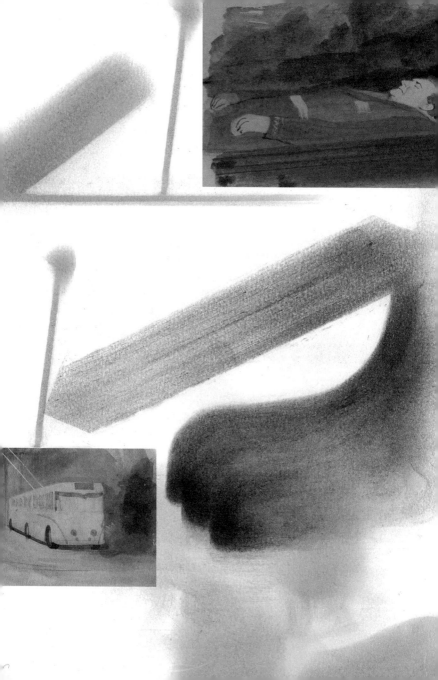

Due to his age, Mr. A. was initially allowed to remain as proprietor of his business, but when he failed to die at an age that conformed to statistical assumptions, he too had to go. He was ordered to cease production — assuming that term can even be used for such sorrowful handicraft — and his duties within the new woodworking enterprise were limited to minor reconditioning and repairs.

"But in your line of work," I said when one day Mr. A. confided in me how he was earning his living now, "I would think that's out of the question."

"That's where you're mistaken, young man," he said. "Not at all! Have you ever seen the products that come out of the cooperative? Nothing but junk, sloppy work, not to mention what gets damaged in transport! And also," he added, lowering his voice, "they don't make coffins for young masters and mistresses anymore, as we used to call them in my day. I can't tell you how many times we have to revarnish overnight. Of course it doesn't add up to a full-time workload, and the customers, well, they're getting more and more demanding every day. Take China, for instance," he said, following his own invisible train of thought. "In China, they're more refined when it comes to paying their final respects . . . But I came up with an idea. An innovation. Home funeral service."

He swallowed a mouthful and washed it down with a gulp from his thermos. "Turned out it wasn't so simple. Who transports bodies from home nowadays? Besides the fact that I don't have a permit. Which is fine," he said, sweeping a few crumbs from his worn black trousers with the stripe down the side. "There's nobody stopping me from walking into a home. Half the time the family members don't even know each other. I just stand off to the side, and naturally I can see right away what's missing, but who would I talk to? I try to scout out a volunteer to organize it. There's always somebody, usually a distant relative, but he doesn't want to disturb the mourners either. Meanwhile the men from the funeral parlor show up, young fellows, who aren't always too respectful. Just screw the lid on and grab the coffin. It can happen — I've seen it!" the old man said excitedly, "— one of the legs on the coffin cracks, or a patch of varnish peels off, or the edging comes unglued while you're attaching the wreath. You think *they're* ready for that? Think again! They don't even know where to begin . . . and that's where I come in. Jumping right in with my tools, lacquer, and glue, dishing out advice like an old hand, and they accept my help, they accept it gladly, like it's understood. The boss can't put me on the invoice of course, but it'd be awkward for them to admit I wasn't with them. They all know me by now. Sometimes they share their tips with me, other times they just pat me on the shoulder, like I was some kind of mascot."

As I stood facing the old man while he readied himself to leave, the wind suddenly kicked up, blowing a poster for some sporting event through the fallen leaves. I breathed deeply, feeling the regular beat of my heart, feeling hungry, and at that moment it was entirely improbable that I would die before him. Noticing my hesitation, he said: "It isn't so bad. The volunteer organizer often offers a token of his appreciation, and sometimes they even insist I join them for a drink. Well, it's been a pleasure. Truly."

We shook hands and the man walked away, but after a few steps he turned and came back to share with me one last thing. "Sometimes it's even funny. If you can imagine, sometimes I'm the first one people come to, to express their condolences. Nice, eh?"

He walked off again, this time at a faster clip, as the wind carried a death knell to us along with a wave of hydrogen sulfide. I followed behind him, slowly, keeping my distance, as it was increasingly inadvisable to be seen in a small group walking behind a priest in his cope, and the time wasn't far off when the church bells would go to rust and the only thing the rope would be good for was for the last crazy bell ringer to hang himself. Otherwise, most people who kill themselves use lighting gas and get taken to the crematorium in Most. The crematorium is cold and damp, and the ovens are heated with semicoke byproduct, which also reeks of lighting gas. Everyone's clothing, even the dead's, is drenched in its cloying odor. Women's hair smells of it too, and the trolleybus seats and conjugal beds and my son's stuffed animals. Death quietly makes its rounds.

III

"TIME GOT AWAY FROM ME," says my neighbor the policeman in a shy, timid voice. "You don't even notice, life is so short. Look at that kid, will you! He's already going to school."

"What, you? You've got plenty of time!" I say.

"Says who? Don't be so sure! Listen," he whispers, "just between you and me, the old ticker ain't what it used to be."

"Well, you'd never guess to look at you!"

"Youth, ha!" he barks with a dismissive wave of the hand. He looks up from beneath his half-closed eyelids, meaningfully, as if keeping a secret, as if he knew something, but it's just one of those habits that comes with being a cop. He doesn't know a thing, it's just the way he's used to fighting for his life. For his right to use the plot he enriched by carting in seven hundred and thirty-six loads of forest soil, for the hope that he will outlive his wife and his vigorous, red-blooded son-in-law, that he will be rewarded and reap all the fruits of his labor.

But he too, I've been told, gets up at night and paces around the house till dawn, leafing through old issues of travel magazines and for the hundredth time rereading articles from *The Gardener's Adviser*. He too, I've been told, sometimes wakes his suffering wife, seized with anxiety, insisting that she help him try to recall the name of his deceased cousin's second husband.

His window shines long into the night, and when I come home late, it evokes in me the illusion of home, that warm, melting feeling in the hollow under my breastbone that I first felt one winter in the early thirties as we made our way home through the muddy streets of Prague after sledding. And, like the aging lawyer, he too often falls asleep only once the alarm clocks ring, sleeps with his mouth open, and in his sleep pronounces names of people no one in his family has heard of.

Thus the crooked monks still haunt the castle ruins at midnight, carrying their chopped-off heads, thus Ahasver wanders eternally, thus Alice always takes to bed at the first sign of a fever, so she can live to see nightfall on the embankment with the bouquinistes. It can happen, there are no signs of impending death. Everyone is as lush and overgrown as a tree in summer. Even the girls whose fine bones ordinarily trace the bare branches of an autumn tree beneath their skin are lush here; they stroll around the square with sacks of candy and chocolate-covered ice cream, scampering from shop to shop, their jaws in constant motion. Life is treating them well.

Life is treating everyone well. Socialism has raised the workers' standard of living. The janitor at school sweeps up two or three crowns a day in ten-heller coins. There are lines to buy meat, people's committees monitor the menu for daycare centers and nursery schools, and they have long since stopped putting crosses on bread, since it isn't a gift from God anymore.

"You know the type, all skin and bones?" says a man over beer. "Listen, comrade, a working man wants something he can grab hold of. She's fat, who cares, let her eat. My old lady, when we tied the knot, she barely weighed one forty. I kid you not, comrade! And look at her now: Seven years we're together and she's up to two oh five, net weight. I keep her well fed."

"Me, on the other hand," says another, a scrawny sort who looks like he suffers ulcers, "me, I've got a boy at home. Little nipper, you know. This is my second old lady. Well, you know the story, now, you know it, right? Young gal! When the kid was first born, it was nothing but little baby blankets and little baby pillows and little baby comforters. Then she starts going to this lady doctor. For consultations. I mean, whatever's best for her, right, as long as the kid doesn't suffer. Well, but then she starts feeding him according to regulations, with a measuring glass and everything, one-fifty, two hundred, know what I mean?"

"Actually, no," says the first man. "We don't want kids. Fundamentally opposed, comrade!"

"Can't argue with that. None of my business, right? But like I was saying, she fed him what the lady doctor told her, and the boy was pale as a ghost, bawling and bawling, all night long. So one day I mix him up a bottle of formula, just plain old Sunar, like all the other kids eat, and the boy sucks it down, man, just sucks it down and reaches out his little hands for more. You want more, you can have it, I say, that's what your daddy earns money for. So I go out and buy some sponge cake and my old lady cooks up some porridge — and what do you think happens, huh? Huh, what do you think? A nice, quiet night, the kid just lying there gurgling, now he's fifteen months old and weighs . . . guess how much, come on! Three ounces shy of thirty-five pounds, comrade. You should see the rolls on his cute little butt. Waiter, another one all around!"

Death makes its rounds unnoticed. Only the old people who can't take the climb to the eleventh floor when the elevators are broken, only the retirees who sometimes, in a fit of lavish spending, splurge on pickled fish and die of a hyperacidic stomach. Death no longer announces itself by the hooting of the barn owl and the little owl, the way it did in the old days, when customs officers chased smugglers through the woods.

It lies in ambush. It's in no hurry. It lives lazily off the past prosperity of mass graves. A few houses away from us lives a family with several children. The father was ill and stayed at home, and as soon as the threat of a visit from Party officials had passed, he turned to cultivating his garden. He planted dwarf trees, prepared the seedbeds, and constructed a rock garden. When spring rolled around, he decided to fence it off. He got hold of some old boards and spent days sawing them into planks about fifteen inches in length. Any big kid could easily have stepped over them. The fence was meant less as an actual barrier than as an indicator of privacy. He put a lot of hard work into it, sharpening the slats with a hand saw and plunging them into the ground, one by one. At the end of each day, he would add a bright green coat of paint to his completed work. There was something disturbing and threatening in the way he went about it.

When he got to the point where he had barely fifteen feet left, our neighbor took to his bed, and a few days later he was dead. I spoke to the family on their way home from the burial. They said he burst a stomach ulcer by pushing the boards against his stomach too hard when he was sawing. Got called off the job.

I'm not making fun. Balzac died the same way, both Pushkin and Mozart left their work unfinished, Zola was found dead over an incomplete sentence. And Michal Mácha too, as we know, found the rough draft of a poem, written in pencil, in the red-lined pocket of his brother the poet's overcoat, still damp from the water that he used to put out the fire in the Litoměřice barns. I write every word with anxiety, here, in this windy room, where the lovers of my youth once kissed, next to the bookshelf that used to have the nest of a wild rabbit behind it, on edge from the muffled banging of the door. I could be interrupted at any moment, even now they are converging on my door from every direction, even now they are giving each other the sign, the chase is on. And my neighbor the policeman bends over a carrot patch right beneath my window, ever the vigilant outpost.

EVEN NOW THEY ARE ARRIVING aboard packed trolleybuses, even now they are jostling for the trains, even now they are kickstarting their 500cc's, even now they are marching in closed ranks with rifles and steel helmets, even now they are placing their children in the baby carriage, even now they are lewdly trying on nylon lingerie in front of the mirror, even now they are stretching the wires from house to house — even now they are forming an impenetrable ring of encirclement.

Every word I write here could be my last, because any key can unlock my door, because the earth is shaking with underground explosions, because every radio and television set could be switched on all at once, this very instant, drowning out the roar of the women in birth and the dying men, because millions of peace doves have been released and the beating of their wings blows through this ramshackle house like the icy wind that ruffled Dante's hair when he found himself standing alone amid the mist and darkness.

They have already measured and weighed me, examined me nude from every angle, probed into every crease of my body and soul, described my special marks, measured the diopter of my shortsighted eyes, counted my hairs as well as my books, objectively and accurately identified from the proper angle the imprints of your opal fingernails on my shoulder, my sweet, they have already predicted the plaintive melody of the laundrywomen on the opposite riverbank and catalogued all my heresies and all my follies, statistically established my need for air, clouds, autumn smoke, freedom and drinking water, and you, my dear Jakub, delight of my life, some imbeciles with the brains of a district school inspector have calculated you as the bones of my bones and entered you in the column marked population growth.

There are no bad moments, or good or better ones, but every moment is the last. Because even now they are on the way; the chase is on and the ring of encirclement has been closed. The bullet with the beautiful name of Atropos has been cast in the course of some sleepy night shift, the withdrawal has been completed, the positions vacated one by one, and there is nowhere left to retreat to.

THE TIME FOR COMPLETENESS IS PAST — because here they come, flat-skulled, slow-witted, braggarts, jokesters, sensible idiots, lustful and lewd, here they come, the youth of the world — my brothers. Coming for me to give them an accounting of all my unearned and squandered money, coming, informers and cruel liquidators, for me to answer their questions out of fatigue, out of loneliness, out of my futile yearning for Florence, out of the coffee that I drank in the early part of the night, out of my childhood and my youth, coming for me to betray my secret to them.

But I have no secrets, the route from the past to the future passes through this room, my door is open night and day, and what I say is so hard to say that my hands are covered in callouses. All that is mine is yours — offered up for the sympathy of the tenderhearted and the laughter of the jokesters. And here is the only thing I have still kept hidden from you — so look, everyone, look closely and listen up! Look so you will have something to talk about when you reach the end of your saliva-moistened thread of stories!

We were coming home from sledding one day when we were children. It was the time of the spring thaw. The runners of our sleds scraped over the muddy cobblestones as we dragged them through the streets. *The Little Reader* had just come out that evening, and I stayed up long into the darkness, reading the story of Carnelian the young alchemist by the light of an arc lamp.

Then one evening, about ten years later, I was saying good-bye to a girl. It was Táňa . . . well, look at that! It's been years since I wrote that name! So there we were saying good-bye when all of a sudden she marched off toward my house, striding over puddles as she huddled against the rain in her plaid yellow coat. When we reached the tram stop, she stood waiting silently, hands in her pockets, a foreshadowing of your own forlorn shivering, until I boarded the tram and rode off. She didn't walk away as long as I could make her out amid the sheen of darkness.

And then, last Christmas in this ghastly town, honeycombed with crumbling mine shafts and tombs, in this house in full view of the world, in this last line of defense, under siege by a patient policeman, my wife told me about how the Jewish girls in Maerzdorf concentration camp used to steal potato peels. She was smiling the whole time and smoking a cigarette. That's all. All that I was still hiding. You have the right to know it, because there are no besieged and besiegers, no persecuted and persecutors. We are all persecuted and we all persecute. Everything is connected, as everyone knows — and we are all brothers, whether you like it or not.

And I say it again and again: This is the future, of our life and of our death.

THIS IS HOW BENDA THE WELDER from the Stalin Works died. Life treated him well. He had a cleanly, hardworking wife, weighed a hundred and seventy-five pounds, and his twelve-year-old girl was as well developed as an eighteen-year-old woman. He kept an aquarium, took photos, served in the auxiliary police and the factory militia. He was a workhorse and a jokester.

On the day of his death, his assignment was to cut through a pipe fifty feet up, so a length of it could be taken out and replaced with an elbow branch. But Benda had found a bundle of signs lying around an office somewhere printed with the instructions TURN TO YOUR SHIFT MANAGER AT NIGHT FOR ALL YOUR NEEDS!

so he strode in for his fatal assignment with his satchel slung over his shoulder, whistling and catcalling at all the women and girls as he handed the signs around. As they squealed with laughter, Benda was already looking forward to bragging about the joke to his buddies at the taproom, where he always stopped in for a few beers standing up at the counter on his way home from the plant.

He was in good spirits as he stepped onto the pipe bridge and set to work. He sat astraddle a broad duct, which gave the women walking by cause for further comment and him the chance for a few choice comebacks in response. The sun shone brightly even through the thick clouds of ash and smoke, the factory pulsed with the rhythm of joyful work, and Benda the welder at that moment was inclined to view this world as the best of all possible worlds. He finished cutting through the tube in front of him and, in the heat of the action, deftly spun around to begin cutting through the other side. Even before he could finish, the heavy, well-fed man went crashing down to the concrete floor and was killed on the spot.

The deputy director of the facility spoke a few words over the coffin, saying that Benda was not only a good worker and politically conscious, but an exemplary and superb representative of the working class. I saw a picture of him, and he looks exactly the same, to the last detail, as the man in the overcoat and cap in the Čumpelík painting *Dawning of a February Day*.

Obviously Benda didn't pose for that painting, but it stands as proof that, for once, the State Prize was awarded to the right man. Our fates take on a new dimension of typicalness when they become the subject of a work of art. Michelangelo painted his own face among the damned of *The Last Judgment*, Dürer lent his likeness to St. Lawrence in the cauldron of boiling oil, and Pushkin predicted his own death by bullet.

So it was that one day, in a sudden burst of sadness, I wrote in red pencil on the marble tabletop of a café in Jindřichův Hradec: *Ici était Robert Desnos le 23 mai 1952* — for at that silent moment, as a gray cat slowly entered through the open door and settled in on an empty chessboard, it was unbearable to think the poet was dead, and that Josef Stuna, who testified to his death, was lost God knows where and I would never set eyes on him again.

Yes, this too, unconsciously, I kept secret from you, even though there was no reason to, since no doubt the waiter wiped away my silly inscription before anyone could get excited about the poet's reappearance. I know it isn't important — but you have the right to know.

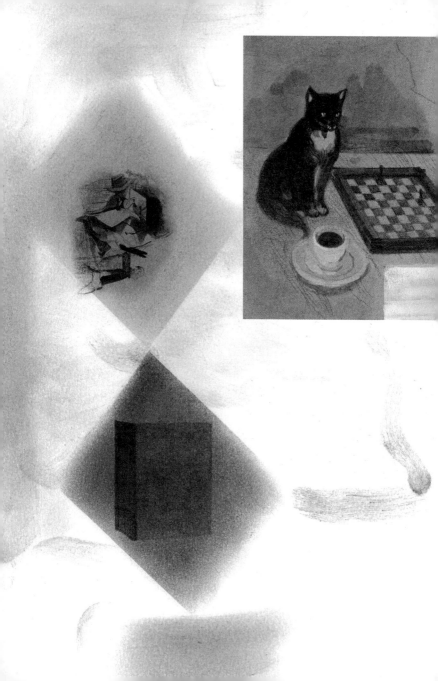

Of course! You have the right to know everything: where the Elbe flows into the sea and the difference between a Doric and an Ionic column. Whether people live on Mars. Which plants are gamopetalous. What electrical induction is and which newspapers my father read. You have the right to know the physiology of Anne Catherine Emmerich's visions, the nine parts of speech and the social-historical causes of Rimbaud's revolts, about the Guelfs and the Ghibellines, Tristan's madness, your hidden birthmarks, and Mendeleev's table of the elements. . .everything. . .everything . . .

And if the telephone rings — as happened some time ago to my wife — and the editor of *Development*, the factory magazine, asks: Tell me, comrade, what is the Latin for death? — there is nothing to do, as you fix your gaze on the impenetrable fog with the trolleys whizzing back and forth and the timid groaning of fauns from within, but answer truthfully: Honor to work, comrade editor! *Mors!*

CONSUMPTION OF THE CHEAPEST variety of coffee beans has increased by nearly a factor of ten over the past three years, according to official statistics. Apparently, a staggering amount of coffee is required for the creation of a new culture. Balzac used to visit several different neighborhoods of Paris to buy his coffee, and created a special blend using his own recipe; Goethe, having an appointment to the court, had no debts and drank wine; Baudelaire took laudanum. But today coffee is an integral part of what in Russia they used to call *priyom*, which is to say method, based in part on the rather fanatical belief that a bedbug can last as long as twenty-five years behind a painting without food. A bedbug, maybe!

One Sunday, Klára Š. and the licensed physician Miloš H. went for a spin on his motorcycle. They drove fifty miles per hour through a series of impossibly kitschy alleys of fruit trees in bloom before turning off onto a road that climbed through the woods into the mountains.

At every switchback, a new and more expansive view opened wide before them, unknown and unnamed, gnawed to the bone by scrapers and bulldozers — the landscape of Klára's life, yet she searched in vain for a glimpse of the window of her office, the road that she took home from work every day, or at least a factory smokestack rising up in friendly greeting from the sea of other, unfamiliar smokestacks.

The road, as it turned out, hugged the border closely, so on reaching the crest they were stopped by a border guard patrol, then again two more times after that, men in uniform surging from the bushes out of nowhere with black dogs straining at the end of their leashes. They parked the 250 in the middle of the junipers, stripped down to their swimsuits, and lay down in the tall grass on the sunny side of a small ravine, exchanging tender caresses. As the sun beat down, the earth exuded the damp smell of spring. Birds cried from the tops of the sparse beeches, while far below, in a vista cut through with barbed wire, a herd of piebald cows grazed. Klára surrendered happily to her companion's gentle touches, her lazy-lidded eyes taking in the grass swaying against the immaculate sky as she breathed in their earthy aroma.

"What's this?" she asked, bending a blade of grass against the man's chest with her tongue.

"Grass."

"Yes, but what is its name?"

He answered with a patronizing kiss. "Grass, just grass. Why? Are you building a herbarium?"

"No. But how can we not even know what the grass is called?"

He sat up and plucked a tiny flower at his feet. "This, if I'm not mistaken, is lungwort: *Pulmonaria officinalis*, formerly used to treat respiratory disorders."

"*Pulmonaria officinalis*? Is that Greek?"

"I don't think so," the young doctor said. "More likely Latin. Do you love me?"

She loved him very much. She loved his stiff hair and clear-blue eyes with their brownish rings of early onset fatigue, his narrow shoulders and boyishly fuzzy chest, his odor of phenol and burnt gasoline. She loved him, and yet as she lay there, head thrown back, gazing up at the red mudguard on his rear wheel, somewhere underneath it all she was also vaguely confused by her desire to be clamped in a dress down to her ankles, hidden within a profusion of corsets and petticoats, which she would have to remove, layer by layer, crushed with shame and thrilled at her audacity.

And then, suddenly, on the verge of losing herself within the adventurous, unfathomable landscape of her body, she had an intimation of a gesture sculpted in marble at the bottom of the sea, jutting into the silence of the fish, desperately reaching out to her, an inkling of the words her tongue, tasting of a smoker's bitter saliva, might have formed, words grand and sweet, all-encompassing, yet long forgotten, and in a split second she grasped how humiliating it is not to be on the same level as one's lover.

"They're watching us!" she cried, suddenly freezing up.

"Oh, baloney. Don't be silly, Klára."

"They've got binoculars. I noticed, they all have them."

"So what? Let them look!" said the man.

As the herd of cows drew closer to the barbed wire, the sound of the tin bells' husky clanging reached their ears.

"Miloš," Klára said again after a moment. "What is . . . immaculate conception?"

He opened his eyes. "For God's sake, why? Is anything wrong?"

"No. I was just wondering. See, when I was a little girl, our grandma told us this story once about an angel that came and . . ."

"An angel?!" said the licensed doctor Miloš H., sitting up.

"Yeah, an angel. You know, with wings. And then Mary . . . she fell to her knees and said: Behold the handmaid of the Lord; be it unto me according to thy word!"

"Handmaid?" asked Miloš Hermann.

"Uh-huh," she said.

"Now listen to me, honey. Number one, we don't have handmaids anymore, so you can forget that. Number two, *Omne vivum ex ovo!* Which means everything living comes from an egg, so this whole immaculate conception thing is obviously just a load of unscientific crap."

"Is that Greek?" asked Klára.

"What?"

"That *omne* stuff . . ."

"No, Latin," said the licensed doctor with certainty.

Because that's what counts, certainty! That's why everyone is so eager to master knowledge. Evening classes at work, college prep, accelerated courses for professional qualifications. Year after year, schooling themselves in Party history and building the foundation of their scientific worldview.

Suspension lamps shine above kitchen tables late into the night as the cruelly humiliated men sit clench-fisted over the printed pages, paging through pocket dictionaries of foreign words and grinding out synopses while their wives dream uneasily of dancing serpents, hands in their lap. They study the spelling reform of Jan Hus and the formula for standard deviation, trying to grasp the difference between Anaximenes and Anaximander and the technology for the manufacture of oxygen by fractional distillation. Enhancing their professional qualifications while assimilating the positive values of society's lower rungs. And in stirring counterpoint to this solitary, secluded concentration, the radio explains the latest innovations in ensilage and the sequence of themes in Tchaikovsky's *Pathétique* symphony, while on TV a thin film of saliva shines between the lips of State Prize laureate Rudolf Hrušínský, playing the role of Tartuffe.

It's the vertigo that comes over me every time I step through the low door into the grand hall of the library at the Strahov Monastery — a pandemic of cultural improvement, the fervor that kept our roommate from Haná up till dawn every night back in the days before February.

She would come home from work around nine o'clock and, still dressed, draw a hot bath. After her bath, she would settle in on the kitchen banquette in a gray robe, eating fruit pastries and smoked meats from home while she read the daily press. Then she would study, plugging her ears, since we were in the next room arguing over the class affiliation of the intelligentsia.

She wanted to begin from the beginning. Alas, neither she nor the humiliated men holding their heads between their clenched fists knew that you can begin and end anywhere.

So she threw herself into Czech grammar. On page one she read that *grammar* was a word of Latin origin, so she went and got herself a copy of Dr. Fürst's high school textbook of Latin. The introduction referred to the civilization of ancient Rome, so she got herself a general history of humanity and spent months trying to digest the chapter on the culture of ancient Sumer and the Akkadian empire. Every time she turned around, a new obstacle cropped up between her and Roman history. Still, she wouldn't give up, studying every day until dawn.

Eventually she was promoted to higher positions and her hunger for knowledge was brought back under control — and while some of us were still wrestling in vain with the question of the intelligentsia's class affiliation, she got married and had a child. I have every reason to believe that everything turned out well for her, and that if she and her family haven't died, they're still alive to this day.

MARRIAGE IS THE CANONICAL happy ending to a story the way that high school graduation is a happy ending to youth. It's just a matter of bringing the syuzhet to a happy end, arriving there through the decelerations of virginal reticence and the digressions of exams. Furnishing the flat. Obtaining qualifications.

Tram stops, train stations, doctor's waiting rooms, everyone studies everywhere. I saw a man reading about medieval mystery plays during the intermission of a variety show with Vlasta Burian.

"You're as loopy as Plato!" the inebriated apprentices mock one another when one of them, after the fifth beer, starts to reminisce about home. And the girls, confiding their cherished secrets in each other, speak of condoms and abortions, salpingitis and fluorine.

Education now belongs to broad swathes of society, along with all the achievements of modern technology.

The district court in Most recently heard the following case: Marie Kondrová filed for divorce from her husband, citing neglect of his husbandly duties and gross bodily harm. The Kondrs have two nearly grown-up children, and up until now their marriage had been by and large a peaceful one.

The breakdown was sudden and unexpected. Břetislav Kondr worked as a maintenance man at the factory. One day the Party officials suggested that he apply for a course of evening classes to prepare for the high school equivalency exam. He submitted all the materials and was accepted. In school, he did his homework and received excellent marks. He devoted all his evenings to study and, as a result, neglected his family. Marital harmony went down the drain.

The tension came to a head in his second year of school. Cultural schematism, the arid approach, mechanistic phraseology, and disrespect for the individual were condemned. The 1941 comedy *Auntie*, starring Jindřich Plachta and Ferenc Futurista, was re-released in cinemas, and the Romantic poet Karel Hynek Mácha was once again taught in schools. So it happened that a young teacher assigned Břetislav Kondr's class the homework of analyzing the themes in Mácha's nineteenth-century masterpiece, the lyrical epic poem *May*.

Kondr worked on his essay until midnight. His wife testified in court that he ignored her calls that dinner was on the table, that he gruffly rebuked her gentle attempts to persuade him, and that he refused to sign their daughter's report card.

"She undressed in front of me in a provocative fashion, then walked around in her underwear, and we've got a twelve-year-old boy at home," Kondr said in his defense.

"No woman should have to put up with that," Kondrová wept. "What does he have to complain about? His shirts haven't had a button missing in his life!"

"Honey, come on," she said that crucial evening. "Give it a break, would you? Please? You're going to drive yourself crazy with all that studying! Besides, I need you to solder the washtub."

"You give me a break, Máňa," said Kondr. "Washtub. I need to know what 'amaranth in springtime sear' means."

"Honey! Please, snap out of it. You never would've talked to me that way before. You were always so good to me!"

"Its weeping sounds from the tomb of all, a horrid yell, a fearful wail," said Kondr.

"It's Jana, you hear me? Our little girl's not a child anymore. Honey!"

"Quiet are the waves, the dark waters' lap, all is covered with an azure cloak; above the water gleams the white dress's shade," Kondr stubbornly carried on, plugging his ears.

"For Christ's sake," Kondrová shouted in court, "it's not every day a girl gets her period for the first time. He's her father after all!"

"Are you gonna give me a break or not, damn it?" Kondr said that evening. "If I get a bad grade on this essay, it's going to mean trouble with the workers' council. And the Party! Karel Hynek Mácha is a major Czech poet of the pre-1848 era."

"Well, Karel Hynek Mácha and the whole workers' council can kiss my ass, you hear? Yes, I broke a plate," she told the court, "but any woman in my place would've lost her temper!"

"She didn't appreciate the importance of my work to society and spoke rudely of a critical workers' organization," Kondr objected. "I was improving my qualifications."

Kondrová knelt on the ground in front of her husband, shouting: "Were things between us that bad before? Tell me, were they? Wasn't our life pretty good? Honey? Look at what nice kids we have!"

"The morning breeze's sweet songlike wafting." Now Kondr was shouting too.

"I'll leave you. I will! I'll take the kids and go wherever my feet take me!"

"Here in the green vale spreads white blossom."

"I'll find some other fella. A hunchback, even, what do I care!"

"There above the woods directs the wild geese's flight."

"Damn it! So you're not gonna stop. You're not gonna stop, huh?!" Kondrová bellowed, yanking the book from her husband's hands and tearing out the pages.

"There bends — upon — the hills — the youthful — saplings!" Kondr bellowed back, striking his wife across the mouth in iambic rhythm, one blow of his fist for each ictus — so she was struck five times, the court learned, corresponding to the iambic pentameter of the verse.

The poem's constructive principle, leaving behind the linguistic material, here becomes a fact of life. As if the slaves from the tomb of Julius II were to shrink back into the stone.

And today, in the final analysis, this is the only possible interpretation that makes any sense. Life puts up no resistance and the material is perfectly malleable. My child outside is playing a pan flute made from a plastic called Stalinite. The material is universal, with no distinguishing features. And the syuzhet practically doesn't exist. The dialectical contradictions have merged in infinite harmony and we can begin and end anywhere. For here truly there is everything — absolutely and without restriction.

ON MAY DAY I SAW the Pioneer bugle corps smartly raise their instruments to their mouths in unison and, gripping their shiny horns in white-gloved hands as they marched past the tribune, they blew a fanfare on the theme of "An die Freude." My son waved a flag, shouting: "Hip, hip, hooray!" An older woman from Lom, who had let us into the first row, said:

"Just look at her! There, Rosenkranzová, struttin' around like a peacock! You know how many parades that woman has marched in in her life? But that's her thing, that's what she does!"

My God! How strictly we used to sort and classify, how urgent and austere it felt, marching hand in hand, shoulder to shoulder, in broad ranks of thirty-two, on an empty Wenceslas Square. It was like love, till death do us part. Like your terrible shivering nakedness in the total presence of love. What good, what good would God be here, if that were even possible? He prepares us for him, with dread and suffering, jealously and vigilantly, for the Antichrist is surely possessed of great beauty and grace, and tempts us with hope of a sweet death. But God is my fortress and my shield, and He shall give neither you to me, nor me to you, lest the salt lose its taste and there be nothing to season with. He shall turn aside our paths, mine and yours. He shall place mistrust, greed, and hatred in our hearts, that we may no longer be tempted by death, but that we may be set apart and reserved for Him, for Him for all eternity. That again and again and always and to the last breath, over and over, we may clench our hands into a fist as we cry the words *No pasarán!*

"And Šlechta there," said the woman from Lom. "He's been carrying that flag like that going on forty years now. He's only got one leg, you know. Thanks to that accident at Kohinoor mine, but now he's having the time of his life. Living it up, yes sir! Look at him, invalid and all!"

"Hello!" my boy shouted, seeing our neighbor the policeman in the crowd. "Hello! Hip, hip, hooray!"

The melody of "Ode to Joy," rising to the soprano register, stripped naked like reality. Not brazenly, in a pink garter and black stockings, but in a casual, every-day way, all method aside. Of course: The dialectical tension resolved itself, ushering in a new golden age of Arcadian bliss, the wolf lying down with the lamb. We were all cleansed of ancestral sin at one fell swoop.

And everyone marched in solidarity, side by side, without distinction. Apprentices from Schönbach with painted ties, razzing the nurses from the dispensary dressed in Marian colors. Miners in historical uniforms and chimney sweeps in fresh-laundered caps. Widows of World War II victims, athletes, schoolchildren with paper doves — all marching and with each joyful stride accomplishing the construction of an "Ode" extrinsic to material. As a gray-blue sky arched above the gathered throng, the dazzling blast of the bugles climbed straight up toward a pale crescent moon — as on the day of eternal recurrence, when the dead man, flank pierced by the tusk of a wild boar, opens — Hallelujah! Hallelujah! — opens his eyes. At that very moment, the trot of a lone horse across Red Square blended with the staccato of the "Ode to Joy" and the naked steel of sabers glinted before the face of the Immortal One.

"Hurrah! Hurrah!" my child cried, waving his little flag at a flock of pigeons, who then took flight, together with all the doves of the world, soaring up toward a gigantic representation of the Spirit, unprecedented in scale. Next, the secretary of the Party regional committee ascended the grandstand, collar trimmed in the color of sacrificial blood, and spoke to us of great victory and great hopes and our one and only Father of all the workers, of the intransigence and cruelty that are love, speaking the language of esoterics, like Hermes Trismegistus, while frenzied mothers tore low-fat frankfurters out of salesmen's hands and the disoriented pigeons went scattering to the four winds. And we clapped our hands and chanted slogans, to keep the celebration going and so never again would there come a night when each of us had to lie down alone, staring into the impenetrable dark in this desolated desert, knowing all too well that it went against reason and all the laws of nature for us to hope that the devil would come and sit at the head of our bed to tempt us.

And besides, it's better not even to wish for it, what with the walls being so thin and the neighbors listening in with their ear pressed to a pot — the devil's complaints, especially when corroborated by witnesses, are viewed as highly suspect in the eyes of the world.

So all we have left is the constructive principle of prose if in the morning we still want to be able to recollect what we looked like the day before, because this is a world of digressions and decelerations, a world of idiotic novellas, embarrassingly intermeshed and unthinkingly devised, a world of prose, an athematic world, without beginning and without end.

There was a time when I still told myself that you would come if I thought of you, if I implored you, my sweet! — there, between the nursery school and the crèche, striding across the dug-up plain with your red-and-white range pole, and that all of a sudden — *courage!* — you would step out of your flowery dress and stand there, stripped to the waist, among the trash cans filled with funeral wreaths and ribbons, and you would sing as birds came flying in from every direction, siskins and goldfinches and wagtails, whose cages, dear love, the young fowler had opened wide in defiance — but today I know you will not come, that you are feeding a child, that you are three hundred crowns short of making it to the next payday, that you are baking cookies and doing your laundry . . . And me, I will go again to close the door that won't shut all the way and opens by itself in the draft, again I will sneak up the creaky stairs to avoid being seen by my guardian angel, again and again — *quand même!*

Yes! Farewell! Farewell, my love! Never, oh, never again will I see you turned to the left staring into the sun, never, oh, never again will you say, hands tucked in the pockets of your plaid yellow coat: You're too caught up in delusional thoughts to be able to see what you could if you threw away your illusions. You aren't living on earth!

No, my dear! I know that this is everything. Absolutely and irrevocably. And, as Chekhov supposedly said, if there is a rifle hanging on the wall, it has to go off by the end of the story.

I know and I testify to the fact that it was for us they spurned the Parma violets and bought the two Italian trolleybuses, for us they built these homes open on every side, so that we could live in them and suffer in them, love each other and make babies in full view of the world, I know that we are, we are, we are the contents of our own story.

We can't take back a word of it now. All of it is as valid and valuable as life itself — here, at this moment, as the universal embryonic material passes through our hands. And once the rifle is already hanging on the wall — Hynek! — Vilém! — Jarmila!

"I BROKE A GARTER," said the woman to her neighbor in line for vegetables, "so I go into the underpass, and just then he comes down the stairs, my old man. Hold on, Miss, he says, I can help you with that! So I smacked him one — and that's how we met."

"Yes, ma'am," says an old lady in sneakers with a cane, "that's fate for you. Not a thing you can do, it's fate every time!"

So there is nothing left but to motivate my athematic prose — here in this ramshackle little house with a draft blowing through from the gaping mouths of the encircling rubberneckers. Of course. Destiny — Ananke . . . Moira . . . Atropos . . . Of course: because this *is* the final battle. *Eto yest nash poslednyi i spravedlivyi boi!*

Because one day the moment will come when Alice gets married and we all realize that the pearly haze of the Paris streets is the color of her wedding dress. Because one day the moment will come (*allons, enfants!*) when men pour onto the ice, cheering and waving their sticks to the delirious fans, the moment (*allons!*) when a man spits blood in a corner of the ring while the women shudder in orgasmic spasms, because it will come, one day too the moment will come when your first love, having comforted a child that isn't yours, withdraws to the bathroom only to reemerge moments later in a white ball gown with a pot of light tea and homemade cookies. One day you will work your way up to foreman after all, one day you will drink fifteen beers for the first time, one day you will sit down and write a book at night, one day you will get married and obtain a driver's license, one day you will take the floor at a meeting and make a speech (*allons!*) about the Great Father of the Proletariat, one day you will denounce your neighbor for his disloyal views, beat your wife and lock your child in a dark room, one day you will realize that you're going to die. No! You cannot outwit fate with love as Eurycleia tried to do!

As for him — he of course knew that the tender rocking in Circe's arms signified return after all — but Alice shouldn't have had any doubt, years ago, staggering down an alley of Corots in the immense halls of the Louvre, that courtship and a wedding wasn't all that there was to it. We should have known that one day young seamstresses would be mending the banner of revolution with their slender thread. It's a terrible thing, returning home to Ithaca in beggar's rags, leaning on a swineherd for support, without ever having seen a set of oars churning the ocean to foam; bending the mighty bow to the breaking point in the general pause that marks the beginning of solitude while knowing nothing of the velocity of the arrow, established once and for all by the curve of Circe's hips. I envy, how I envy Alice that dark amateur photo she has of herself leaning against the railing of the Eiffel Tower in the wind; I envy you sometimes seeing projected on the X-ray screen the subtly traced bronchial tubes of the French repatriates, sprinkled with coal dust from somewhere out near Charleville. There are several dozen of them here, French and Belgian miners who came home after '45 with a foreign accent and silicosis. They cough beneath my window, wheezing on the trolleybus and in line to punch the clock. Microscopic particles of dust and whitish soil swirl about the pestilent air of Compiègne, that "land fat and yet infertile, a land of flint and chalk." Occasionally they exchange a few words in French, which I don't understand. I search their wrinkles for traces of the salty ocean air and greedily inhale at least the chalky smell of their dry coughs. The only reality of desire.

> *Somewhere between l'Hay-les-Roses*
> *And Bourg-la-Reine and Antony*
> *Among the roses of l'Hay*
> *Between Clamart and Antony . . .*
> *Chalk and flint — chalk and flint . . .*

And chalk . . .

They hide their secrets. Fermenting rose hip wine, planting their gardens with artichokes and curly lettuce, which they harvest only after the first frosts, their wives appearing out of nowhere in nylon blouses of exotic cut, holding raucous wedding parties with the same scratched Piaf records playing over and over. Sometimes one of them succeeds in jumping through the hoops, getting a passport and a visa to visit their dying mother — and they leave, maybe aboard the mythical Prague–Strasbourg–Paris–Calais express, thereby testifying to the reality of the improbable.

Because the statute of limitations on old testimony is running out. When Alice took her trip to Paris, the homes in Litvínov were nearing their completion and the plot where my neighbor's crocuses are poking up their heads was still covered in pine needles, deer droppings, and the tiny bones of dead birds. Meanwhile the People's Republic of China celebrated victory, work was launched on the grandiose task of transforming nature, and the nation's biography was revealed in a series of Party purges. Meanwhile the children shouting outside my doorstep right now were born, the apprentices left the boarding school, and the Collective House took in its first tenants. Henri Martin was put in prison and the song about the dockers' strikes was added to French lesson plans. Paul Éluard died, and so did André Gide, and the Kondrs divorced, and the Pomykal family's injuries healed, and Klára Šnajdrová gave birth to the child she had so maculately conceived, and my wife also felt her baby move for the first time on May Day 1952, without our even noticing, amid the clapping in time to the chanting, that it was Walpurgis Night, and the Korean War ended, and the observation tower on Petřín Hill was transformed into a television transmitter, and Slánský died with a noose around his neck, and Benda the welder achieved immortality, Stalin died and four tender young lieutenants, ammo pouches filled with Pushkin, Rimbaud, and Hemingway, laid the thinly smoking coffin to rest on a sarcophagus in the mausoleum on Red Square, a plane carrying the national hockey team crashed into

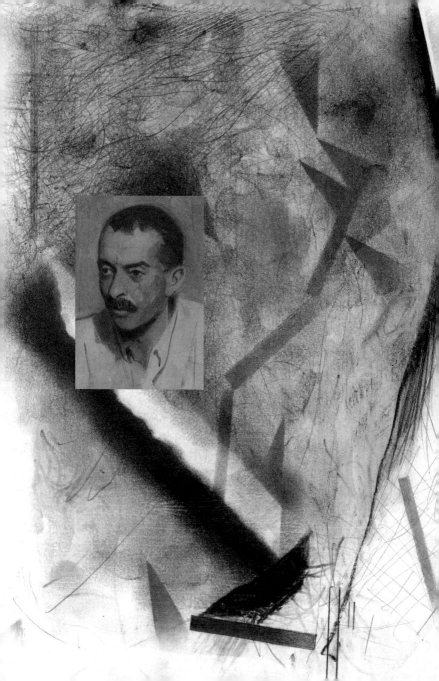

the Atlantic, Picasso painted his dove and Max Švabinský his portrait of Julius Fučík, and the old lawyer succumbed to dementia, and E. F. Burian was named colonel, and the remains of Velehrad were discovered, and new types of canned meals appeared on the market.

AT THE END OF OCTOBER, Comrades Khrushchev and Tito went deer hunting in the forests of the Caucasus. In a spirit of friendly cooperation, they bagged several outstanding specimens, including a twelve-point buck. Owing to a slight indisposition on the trip south, Comrade Bulganin was unable to join the expedition until they reached the peaks.

The infection spread. Europe was racked with the hacking cough of a smoker who hasn't slept a wink all night. The temperature dropped. Crowds of people stood waiting at trolleybus stops as transportation between the housing estate and the factory ground to a halt.

Gingerly, men cupped damp cigarettes in their hands, like their most secret fear from the war. Ladislav Pachta stood, briefcase in hand, in a new-looking brown leather jacket, his tire-tread soles imprinting themselves in the thin layer of mud. He smiled, oblivious in his own private atmosphere of aftershave, soap, and mouthwash.

Meanwhile the training in Melbourne continued. The sun sank red into the white ocean foam, and after a light supper Zátopek and Jungwirth went out for one more run around the dew-soaked grass track.

Heavy drops of cloudy water formed on the trolley cables, rolling toward the insulators and falling off at regular intervals. Everyone silently fed their hope, shivering in the cold.

Ladislav Pachta's wife, waiting with him in gray galoshes, raised a hand to her soggy hair in an unexpectedly dainty gesture, because the fog murmured through the tree stumps like a tide of nylon lingerie, and the horns of the buses in the distance, feeling their way forward step by step in the yellow beams of their headlights, were like the bleating of long-haired Australian sheep with wool of mauve and petrol blue and salmon pink and honey yellow and turquoise, which only looks good on very light blondes.

"Where you off to, Láďa?" asked a man in the crowd.

"Prague. Why do you ask?" said Pachta, stamping another tire mark in the mud.

"Seen your suitcase," said the man. "Genuine leather?"

"Yep, pigskin," said Pachta.

The man lit up a cigarette and offered his open case.

"Not me, I quit," said Pachta. "Or wait a sec! Today being special and all, I'll take one," he said, "on credit!"

"No sweat, it's just one lousy cigarette!" said the man.

"One here, one there, it adds up," said Pachta as his neighbor gave him a light, and he suddenly realized with satisfaction that his unexpected urge for a smoke, awakened after so many years, was proof that our hope isn't all in vain and that life has meaning after all.

"This is a historic moment," Comrade Imre Nagy declared on a square in Budapest. "This is about us and the future of our children!"

The masses cheered and removed their hats to sing an old song from the revolutions of 1848. And as a youthful student holding a satchel and a violin case attempted to sing the "Marseillaise" in a high, shaky voice, armored cars filled with government soldiers in steel helmets rumbled across the bridge over the Danube.

A vibration ran through the cables, spraying the crowd with drops like a sudden downpour. The trolleybus emerged from around the bend.

"I don't know," said Pachta. "The way it looks, I'm going to miss my lousy train!"

Elbowing his way on board, he said, "I got a voucher for a car, a Spartak. I'm on my way to pick it up now."

He pushed his way through to the exit. The cigarette was making him a little dizzy.

Ladislav Pachta had given up smoking eleven years ago, when he met Miluška Mizuňová. She was wearing a turquoise sweater, and even though it wasn't pure wool it looked good on her, since she was young and very blonde.

Long before Sophia Loren ever appeared in cinemas, Miluška had had a weakness for sweaters, but in those days there was no wool to speak of. Still, somehow Pachta, who made a good salary, managed to get his hands on a genuine American pullover. She put it on right away in the entryway of their building, and didn't discourage him from watching.

"You see!" Miluška said. "At least it's good-looking and has some lasting value. What have you got to show for that cigarette? Your money goes up in smoke, and on top of it you ruin your health. Not that I mean to criticize you," she said. "I'm not asking for anything, but take a look at yourself!"

He took her virginity that night, standing against the railing beside the railroad track, and partly out of love, partly out of guilt — because he ruined her kilted skirt, but also because he recognized the logic to her point of view — he gave up smoking and bought himself a covert cloth suit in chocolate brown. That marked an end to the era of infantile disorders and the dawning of the age of mature masculinity, which isn't afraid to set long-term goals.

And why not? Pachta thought. Eleven years! And with a feeling of contentment, he felt his coursing blood wash away the last traces of queasiness.

"Maybe I might get a lift sometime!" said the man with the cigarettes when Pachta got off. Then he turned to his neighbor good-naturedly, with no envy in his voice: "We're still saving up for a TV set. Yeah, must be all that sewing his wife brings home!"

In front of the textile mill by the train station, Pachta ran into a young man dressed in the uniform of the factory militia.

"Honor to work!" he said, giving the official Party greeting.

"Honor!" said Pachta. "What gives?"

The young man shrugged: "Alert!"

In a kibbutz on the shore of the Lake of Genezareth, meanwhile, girls with black eyelashes practiced throwing live hand grenades. The exercise was held under the command of a woman with short-trimmed gray hair and a number tattooed on her left forearm, who turned away every time a grenade accidentally landed in the lake's blue waters and dead fish floated to the surface, belly up, baking white in the sun.

The train stank of urine like an old woman in need of a bath. Ladislav Pachta stepped into a half-empty compartment. Three men were playing a game of cards in the corner. He sat down on the seat opposite, watching indifferently, with no comprehension, from inside his private bubble of hygienic perfumes. He had a vague recollection that the ten of diamonds meant money, but they weren't using a tarot deck, so that wasn't any help.

Pachta didn't play cards. Eventually, after he and Miluška bought themselves an American kitchen, stainless steel silverware, and service for six and got married, he also stopped going to the pub, and stayed at home to drink his weekly Sunday beer.

"The most important thing," said Miluška after the wedding, "is a nice polished living room. But not just any ordinary one. In that case, I'd rather have nothing. In that case, I'd rather wait. And proper upholstery, horsehair, lasts a lifetime. Sit down in your chair, turn on the radio, and what more do you need? Home," said Miluška. "Nothing beats a beautiful home."

The world was overflowing with fine, soft, shiny, polished, and mechanical things, bulldozers dug up ground for new housing estates, rivers were engineered and dams erected, tracks were laid for new railroad lines, factories blazed at night with a thousand lighted windows, and consumption of meat, flour, fat, electrical appliances, and textiles rose to staggering heights. The market abounded in an ever-growing variety of new products, the Petřín observation tower was transformed into a television transmitter, motorcycle prices were slashed, and the first popularly priced automobiles appeared on the roads. The outlook on life was breathtaking.

They saved up for a floor lamp, a camera, then a radio-gramophone and a wringer washing machine. It was a perfect marriage right from the start. Miluška made good money sewing, and she knew how to economize.

"You shouldn't cut corners on food," she would say, "but if we buy a pound of meat, we have to make up for it somewhere else. If you're still hungry, fill up on bread and butter."

"Truth is," she said, counting her money one payday, "we could have had it all long ago. But you got stuck, Láďa, sorry to say. Look at Kondr! He's improving his qualifications, and soon he'll be foreman. That's three hundred more a month, at least."

So Pachta also started classes at the technical school four nights a week. He would sit up until midnight, head between his fists, poring over logarithm tables and *A Brief History of Czech Literature*, while the teary-eyed Miluška pedaled away at the sewing machine. He worked his way up. They bought themselves a TV set and he was asked to join the Party.

Next, they began saving for a refrigerator and a Jawa 250. Their standard of living continued to rise. The only thing Miluška didn't want was children.

"There will be plenty of time for children once we've got it all," she said when he brought it up one day. "Lucky nothing happened back then, when we were young and stupid."

Even before the wedding, she procured a large box of condoms and tested them all, one by one, underneath the faucet.

"My little dicky," she would say in bed twice a week, "had better make sure he's got his hood on nice and snug!"

But having read in a guide to married life that no method of contraception was 100 percent reliable, she always ran straight to the bathroom afterward to rinse herself out with vinegar water as Ladislav Pachta drifted off to sleep.

I'll stop into a milk bar for a deviled egg, Pachta thought as he fell asleep on the train. There really is such a thing as luck in life.

He dreamed that Miluška was sewing something in the fog on her machine. She had her wool-blend turquoise sweater on. "Miluška," he called to her. And again: "Miluška!" he shouted. But she just went right on sewing without turning to look, and he suddenly realized that it wasn't fog, but she was on the other side of a window covered in frost. He proceeded to start wiping the glass, panting and sweating heavily, until finally it dawned on him that the pane was made of milk glass, like the windows on pharmacy doors.

He didn't wake up until the train pulled into Prague. His pants were rumpled, his head ached, and his craving for deviled eggs had passed. In Prague it was raining.

An armed uprising had broken out in Budapest. "This is the final battle, let each stand in his place," sang the women and men locked in cellars where the police were lobbing hand grenades. In the lobby of the Hotel Astoria, nine men with severed heads sat silently in easy chairs.

On his way to the automobile dealership, Pachta stopped at a toy store and bought their child puppets of a doggy and a pussycat. Their fifteen-month-old little girl was named Marcela, and she was conceived the day they brought home their chrome-plated Jawa.

That evening they went for a ride around the housing estate, crickets grinding in the meadows, steam rising from the water-filled mines. Miluška laughed as they passed beneath the flowering branches, and Ladislav Pachta had to close his eyes against the shower of apple blossoms.

"In summer it'll be a nice ride over to Litoměřice for apricots," said Miluška, brushing a wilted blossom from the mudguard with her finger. "Every now and then a girl gets an urge for apricots," she said suggestively, adjusting her garter. "Everything costs money. You know that, Ládík."

"Miluška!" he said that night in bed.

"Yes, honey?"

"Sometimes I can hardly believe it's true."

"What?" said Miluška through the hair curler in her mouth.

"How lucky we are."

"You silly little thing!" she said, stroking his thinning hair.

The aria from *Rusalka* played from a radio on the other side of the wall, and the red stars glowed in the dark above the mining towers.

"Maybe we aren't meant to have it all," he said.

"All?" Miluška burst out laughing. "Boy, you don't have any sense of the future at all, do you? Not a lick."

"Miluška!"

"Uh-huh?"

"Do you love me?"

"Of course, sweetie," she said. "Let's start saving up for a Spartak."

Then, as he took her in his arms and pulled her close, she wriggled out of his embrace, removing his condom and laying it on the nightstand in a single tender gesture, while the siren in the distance wailed to signal the start of the third shift.

"C'mere, little daddy," she whispered. "My little daddy."

When Miluška was in her fourth month, they put an end to their outings and sold the motorbike for a profit. Miluška got hold of a layette for next to nothing, they'd socked away seventeen thousand already by the end of her postnatal period, and when little Marcela turned a year old, in recognition of his exemplary and reliable performance, Ladislav Pachta received a special bonus and a voucher for a brand-new automobile.

"Good luck now," said the salesman at Mototechna as Pachta started up the coffee-brown Spartak. "And easy on the shifting till she's broken in!"

He drove off into the rain, cautiously picking his way through the side streets. A head or two turned to look. The car smelled of new leather and paint, and for a moment Pachta's nausea from the morning reappeared. Dusk fell, the shop windows shining brightly as he passed, filled with polished living rooms and radio-gramophones, canned pineapple, Hungarian sausages, gleaming refrigerators, washers and vacuums.

He passed crystal kitchen cabinets, folding cameras, hand-stitched shoes, prams with eight-spring suspension, television sets, and everything and everything, and all of it was the past. Women's torsos shone dazzling white in the twilight, clothed in mauve and honey-colored wool, in salmon-pink nylon with black lace and rayon white as sea foam, in shimmering taffeta and black tulle and Chinese silk the color of turquoise, which only looks good on very fair blondes. Finally Ladislav Pachta steered his chocolate Spartak onto the entrance ramp for the highway. It was pitch dark. He turned on the wipers and switched on his high beams.

Meanwhile in a dark street in a suburb of Budapest, a man stood with his back to a wall that bore the fading inscription *Da zdravstvuyet Krasnaya armiya*. Three militiamen raised their rifles. The man groped awkwardly at the plaster behind him, then opened his eyes wide.

Ladislav Pachta stepped on the gas and plunged into the darkness encased in his capsule of chocolate brown, filled with the smell of leather and hygienic perfumes.

And the training in Melbourne continued. The morning star faded in the east as Zátopek and Jungwirth bounded out onto the sand. The ocean was calm, the waves lapping tamely at their white track spikes.

There was a fog rolling in, low to the ground. Pachta stopped on a hill overlooking the housing estate. He realized he hadn't even taken a good look at the car yet. He got out and walked around the vehicle. The tires had left a clear trail in the thin layer of mud, extending backward from the rear wheels, far into the darkness, on the other end a dazzling white woman's torso with the bust of Sophia Loren, clothed in a turquoise sweater. Pachta started coughing. The infection was spreading.

I'm getting old, he thought, and suddenly his stomach heaved at the memory of the cigarette he had smoked waiting for the trolleybus that morning. He leaned back against the car body for support and, taking great care not to damage the paintwork, vomited a thin stream of acid from his stomach. The Spartak sat there, cool and shiny, at the very center of the world.

"Now we have it all!" Ladislav Pachta said out loud, and he held his breath a moment in the quiet of the dark.

That night a squadron of Soviet planes, with a five-pointed red star painted on their wings and rudders, took off from a Black Sea air base and dropped bombs on residential districts in Budapest.

"Everything," he cried.

And the Spartak sat on the hill overlooking the housing estate, new, unsullied, shiny, smelling of leather and paint; our hope, a refuge for the afflicted, a morning star, an ivory tower, our hope — and beyond it there was nothing, nothing except the infinite universe, empty and desolate, an icy wind blowing through it from pole to pole.

And many began to claim that the photo of Alice squeezing her skirt between her knees in the wind on the top floor of the Eiffel Tower was too blurry to be authentic. Alice fiercely maintains that, whatever they may think, it *is* the pearly haze of the Parisian air, and to prove it she stands up, opens her wardrobe, and shows everyone her wedding gown, stained with a few tiny spots of red wine. And I, despite it all, I still believe what she said, because I know that opalescent light well — I know it from a dream, a waking dream that haunted me often in the first years of the fifties, when the Prague streets spasmed in pain like a snake stripped of its skin.

IV

THE STATION CONCOURSE, THE SAME ONE where Rimbaud once caught the train to Belgium with Verlaine, buzzes and smells like the first day of summer vacation. Then suddenly, imperceptibly, it changes into a covered arcade, filled with cigarette smoke despite a steady draft. Young beardless men crowd the space in pastel-colored suits, cigarettes glued to the corners of their mouths in gold holders. They stand absorbed in the buttons and levers of slot machines with curved glass fronts. The arcade is endless. I hurry along, while in real life Alice stops and wins a flask of perfume from one of the machines. It still has its smell to this day. *Bonjour, monsieur!* I say to one of the young men, but clearly he doesn't understand, continuing to stare tensely off into the endless depths of the arcade. It isn't a dream about Alice; Alice *was* at the Gare de l'Est. The next thing I know, I walk out into the open air and spread before me, against all probability and counter to all expectations, is a delightful landscape in brownish hues, sloping gently down toward the river on whose opposite bank grazes a herd of cows. It's a scene from Corot, complete with hoarsely clanking cowbells. The first thing everyone does, they say, is look for the Eiffel Tower: jutting up in the distance, beyond the bluish haze of the river, above the geode of rooftops. Alice, lugging her heavy suitcase, dodges a water cart. The water wipes away all traces. Stucco facades. LES APPAREILS PHOTOGRAPHIQUES — Alice swears this is the first sign that catches your eye. The jagged rooftop edges. The terrifying, edible beauty of the *style moderne* . . . And I missed some tram or other and I'm wandering along the outer boulevards. The shop windows are filled with prostheses, votive pictures, and ladies' lingerie.

"And that one there is my first wife. A Parisian!" says the janitor from our grade school as he mends the frayed cuff on my everyday trousers.

"What was her name?" I ask, for hope never abandons a man entirely.

"Nadia!" he says with the thread between his lips.

Of course! I know, I know! You won't come! It's absurd. But in my dream I search for you feverishly. I come to New Sorbonne Street: A slim gentleman in a top hat is lighting a cigar for a portly shorter gentleman with a beard à la Napoleon III. *Au revoir, monsieur*

Atget! It's absurd. I'll never run into you. The street is barricaded. I retrace my path, revisiting all the familiar sites. *Au revoir, monsieur Atget!* And suddenly a recess appears amid the blue buildings, as deep as it is wide, a dwelling that deviates from the regulation plan. (There used to be several such buildings in Žižkov when I was a child, and we would hide inside the random niches, shining flashlights in each other's eyes.)

I shudder in sweet amazement: Standing in the recess is the only false acacia the entire length of the street, parched and roundly trimmed, its slender trunk hemmed inside a wire cage. It lasts only a few seconds. The recess in the row of buildings on the outer boulevard, the tree with the rounded crown and the wire cage. I hope to see it again at the hour of my death. What do I care about you and the bullet you cast for me on that sleepy night shift!

The door opens again and a draft rattles the window frames. The swans drink long and thirstily. Two little girls walk beneath my window, singing: Hey, diddle, diddle, the cat and the fiddle, the cow jumped over the moon. Somebody kick-starts a motorcycle. A rain begins to fall and the pile of ash they forgot to haul away oozes hydrogen sulfide. Darkness sets in, and in the Latin Quarter the lights come up behind the red-and-white striped blinds.

And meanwhile, somewhere on the plain between the factory and Litvínov, the trolleybus carrying the workers to their shift has come to a stop. Everyone is still asleep, hanging openmouthed from the grimy handrail, leaning against the mud-spattered window with drops of rain streaming down it. In quiet bliss, a drunken miner vomits down the front of his overcoat with the buttons on the woman's side.

"So are we going to sit here all day?"

"Just as long as they get their money, that's all they care about!" gripes an old woman with an armful of big black bags. "Sixty hellers for two stops. And they call that a zone! They know what they're doing, all right!"

"No juice," says the driver, lighting a cigarette.

"Everyone off," says the conductor, dropping his consonants as he speaks through the needle he's using to clean an aching tooth.

Slowly they wake up, coughing as a wave of chalk carries to them on the wind — ah, the soil of Compiègne. In Paris, near Bourg-la-Reine, I left my love on her own. Let the sirens cradle her to sleep. I sleep easy, oh, my love! . . . The driver presses the button to open the pneumatic doors and the passengers go stomping off through the watery mud, while the drunk miner launches into an unintelligible rant and an adolescent boy with a beret jammed down over his joined

eyebrows, in a feeble and meaningless gesture, spits on the wet windshield in front of the driver.

"All this water, good Lord, it's terrible, so much water!" the old lady with the black bags grumbles to herself. "And nothing but whores and floozies! Whores and floozies, all of 'em!"

"Yes, of course, that's me," says Alice. "Yes, at the Eiffel Tower, that's Paris down there. You can't see it too well, since it's just an amateur photograph. The whole thing was like a dream. He took me around the museums and the quais and Montmartre, but he didn't kiss me even once . . ." And that's the way it always is. The first half of the story.

A man wakes to the clanging of alarm clocks. As a child I always wished that Friday had never come to the desert island, that the ship with clothes and weapons had never shipwrecked, that the Spanish buccaneers had never turned up and Robinson could have spent the rest of his life with the llamas, parrot, and turtles, sheltered away in his cave with the rope ladder. A child doesn't understand, and can't, that the shot from the *Aurora* is just the beginning of everything. That Ulysses awakes in dread on the rocky coast of Ithaca, that Alice weeps standing before the wedding officiant in her gown the color of the Parisian air. He doesn't understand that you too, comrade, are getting old, that the stretch marks on your lower abdomen are widening. That motivation is finished and the battle with the suitors is still yet to come.

And the story continues. Relentlessly. Into infinity. The thrushes have made a nest among the ribbons on the fir tree that the builders raised atop the second wing of the Collective House, still under construction. The children have made their first scratch in the writing bureau varnish. The TV set is broken. Every night a new stream of virginal blood flows. There is still a light ring on the table from when Jeníček was just a little boy and put a hot mug down on it. And here, look at Olinka crying because somebody tore the leg off her teddy bear, the one she slept with every night until the age of four.

And there is no way to stop. In the end you would just be a laughingstock, with your spinster's life of sour spirituality! There is no way to remain in a state of original innocence, given the staggering pace at which resources are being depleted and consumed. Automation is devouring everything: the past and love, metaphor and fashion, joy, pain, marriage, dreams, images, books, music, work . . . A can of ashes, dear! And we have no choice. Again the night lights up unstoppably, again dawn comes irrevocably, the alarm clocks ring and the whole thing starts all over again.

The clock is five minutes slow. Your stocking has a hole in it. The gas pressure is low and the men are shaving with cold water. There's no more toothpaste. The elevators are out of order. It's freezing. Children in sweat suits doze in front of the closed door of the nursery school. A man in blue coveralls runs a limp flag up the flagpole, steel cable screeching. The sewer is clogged and dirty water bubbles up in the middle of the road. Tousled girls in their rented rooms pull up the blinds with a clatter. A yellowed leaf drops from the fig tree in the corner of my room. I feel a stabbing pain near my heart. Remember, for God's sake, hurry up and remember!

Nothing but the present! Trolleybuses, buses, trucks, and trams careen downhill toward the factory, shining out of the fog like a city. The six tones of the time signal beep across the barren landscape and we all adjust our watches. A lighted window glimpsed amid the buildings' gray facade, standing behind it a young woman, arms raised, brushing her hair.

Five thirty, November eleventh, nineteen fifty something. Not the quais of the Seine, not the Luxembourg Garden, not the Pont des Beaux-Arts — but the high-pressure column and the laboratories and the Winkler generators and the evaporation tower, the carbonized path tread by a drunken saxophonist, the distillation and ammonia pipes, the cistern and the watchtowers and the barbed wire and the coaling and the phenols and the pyrocatechol, the deserted desolation, the Stalin Works, a mass grave churned over by backhoes and bulldozers, this world — the hope, the hope, the hope of the world.

BECAUSE THIS TIMELESSNESS can't last eternally. I pound some more nails into the walls of this model home, and the edges of the stairs crumble into a fine dust as we walk up and down them. Yesterday I slapped you across the face, Jakub, my darling, so that you would honor your father and mother and all would be well with you on earth. A fine ash from the power plant smokestacks settles onto book edges and grinds between our teeth, people die before our eyes, and we go to funerals. We cut down the tree growing under our windows. And our faces look more and more like our death masks will someday.

I haven't been writing this prose in vain. What do you all want from me? What do I care about you and your literature? I don't understand you and I've got nothing in common with you. Except fate. And I predicted your future.

Look! Over there, coming down the slope from the club for Stalin Works personnel, it's Daphnis Kučera the mining apprentice. He's staggering a little, having consumed two steins of strong beer and two shots of rum on an empty stomach. His necktie blazes with color between the lapels of his jacket, and the evening star is rising in the pale sky overhead. He stumbles through the broken bricks, rusty cans, and nettles.

And here, walking toward him, down an alley of truncated chestnuts still fluttering with some tattered May Day streamers, comes Chloe Drexlerová, a spinner at the textile mill. She stops and straightens the seams on her nylons with one of her black high heels. She is stout-legged, with round knees, and turning red in the face under the burden of her breasts, weighing her down, pulling her closer to the dead.

From far away you can hear the loudspeakers broadcasting a bulletin from the local radio station and the drawn-out voices of mothers leaning out windows calling their children, who are outside scaring away the fauns and dryads with their shouts. Time to come home now! Hurry up! We're turning on the TV! An emergency ambulance drives past, its siren wailing menacingly.

And the two of them meet on the muddy roadway, lined with sections of big black gas pipe, so that in the future too there will be enough heat for a nighttime cup of coffee and enough sweet hissing silence for death.

"Hey there!" says Daphnis. "Took you long enough!"

"You reek of rum," says Chloe.

"Yeah, so?"

"So nothing. My uncle came by, so I got held up."

"Which uncle?"

"Which one do you think?"

"Listen, Chloe, I get the feeling he's — you know — with your mom, no?"

"Probably."

"Aren't you the naughty one!" Daphnis laughs out loud.

Chloe shrugs and pulls her coat tightly around her body.

"Little girl like you ought to believe that babies come from storks."

"You mean they don't?" says Chloe.

"No, the crows bring them."

On the other side of the wooden fence a child blows a panpipe, and far away, far out of sight, a hut of mastic branches squats beside an azure bay. At any moment, without warning, this place, like any other, can become the stage for our dying and our death. So it is that even Oedipus Rex himself descends from the universality of myth into the columns, broom flowers, and olive pits of the lowly cothurnus of tragedy.

"I don't like when you talk dirty!" says Chloe.

"And I don't like when girls act prissy! But nice suit you got. What'd it cost you?"

"Four hundred for the fabric, three for the sewing. But it's genuine tweed. S'posedly it's the next big thing. That's what this girl I work with says whose cousin lives in France."

"Maybe he could send her over a 2CV?"

"I don't know, maybe not, he's just a distant cousin . . . But can you imagine, Daphnis, me in a car, pulling up to the factory in the morning? I've already got the tweed for it."

"I could be your chauffeur. You don't know how to drive anyway. Gals never . . ."

"Ow! Let go!"

"C'mon, Chloe!"

"Let go, I said! Quit fooling around!"

He presses her up against the fence, trying to kiss her. The young woman stands eyes closed, arms at her side.

"First time a gal's laid that one on me, goin' stiff as a log."

Chloe gives Daphnis a slap in the face and runs off in tears. A song pours out of the loudspeaker on the utility pole above their heads, drowning out Daphnis's shouts. He takes off after her, tripping over twisted wires and baby carriage carcasses, until finally he catches up and knocks her to the ground between the wilted nettles and a tattered mattress in a corner of the enclosure.

"No, no! Please, no!" sobs Chloe.

"C'mon, Chloe!" Daphnis shouts over the roar of the loudspeaker. "In six months my apprenticeship'll be over. We can get married and find a flat somewhere."

"It's me, me, young liberty, a red-petaled flower, blossoming free," blares the loudspeaker above their heads, and the young woman cowers under the onslaught of the song. The two of them thrash about, her heels churning up the soil, giving off a raw odor of roots and tar. Every few seconds the headlights from a passing automobile shine through the cracks in the fence. Then the song ends and suddenly there is silence, deep, infinite, and boundless as the sea.

Chloe slowly raises her arms, with the motion of a bird taking flight, the tips of her fingers momentarily aiming at the evening star, then crosses them over Daphnis's head, and lowers them in an embrace of north and south, an instant of joy at the heart of life, a second of existence in harmony and free of torment, dwelling within the vast expanse of hope.

"Listen, Chloe, love of mine," whispers Daphnis, "they're building new flats in Zahražany. We can put in a request for one and be together. We can be together forever and to hell with everything else. I'll support you, Chloe. I can do it. Anyone can earn a living these days!"

They don't know yet that this too is actually infidelity, this too is a fall, they know nothing about me, leaning out the window of this drafty room overlooking the wasteland at this critical hour, at this hour when the world hangs on our fragile silence, theirs and mine, that it's virtually no longer allowed to touch things that don't rend and tear, to hunt for a door that's still open, to recollect the azure cove with its hut of mastic branches, carpeted with moss and periwinkle; they have no idea yet that, midway upon the journey of our life, the only precious thing fate leaves us with is this stone overgrown with thyme . . . this barbed wire slicing across the morning sky . . . and a girl's breasts trembling under the bursts of the Fifth Symphony . . .

"Do you love me?"

"Yes."

"And will you always love me?"

"Always."

"And will you never forget me?"

"No. Never ever!"

AND THE STORY CONTINUES. There is no other way out. Slowly the pain matures, the pain for which a place has been reserved in our breast since we were born. That final hesitant gesture of the hand coming to rest on the heart is ripening even now, just as the pain itself has been ripening for as long as we can remember, through small, subtle, nearly imperceptible injuries, through memory, hope, betrayal, fear, with each hot cup of coffee and cigarette, everything heading toward it and it alone, we all belong to pain — long before it brutally seizes us in its agonizing grip. We are halfway through life and the story continues. Farewell!

Farewell, Táňa, farewell, Eva, farewell, Jiřina, farewell, Slávka and Zdeněk and Hanka and you who have no name, farewell! Farewell, my love! Farewell!

We can begin and end anywhere, but the only thing that still matters is the interpretation of the journey. Farewell, farewell, my love!

Again the door has opened and a draft blows through this house of our hope, of our life and our future, like the wind that ruffled Dante's hair when he found himself standing alone amid the mist and darkness . . .

Litvínov 1954–1957

During the 1960s, numerous 'texts of disillusion' were published in Czechoslovakia by writers like Ivan Klíma, Milan Kundera, Dominik Tatarka and Ludvík Vaculík, who, often as students, had supported the 1948 Communist takeover and gone on, to differing extents, to serve the Communist Party or work within its structures. Josef Jedlička's *Midway Upon the Journey of Our Life*, dated as written between 1954 and 1957, is considered one of the earliest examples, and foreshadows many of the themes perhaps most familiar to international readers from later Kundera novels. No other text in the period, however, goes further than Jedlička's in its uncompromising indictment of Czechoslovak Stalinism in practice, its expression of the culpability of intellectuals, and its still resonant characterization of the experience as symptomatic of a broader, destructively materialist direction taken in twentieth-century Europe.

Unlike many of his contemporaries, Jedlička left the Communist Party soon after the takeover, by the autumn of 1948. As a result, he lost his place at university and struggled to find meaningful work, and in late 1953, he moved from his native Prague to the north Bohemian industrial town of Litvínov, the setting of *Midway Upon the Journey of Our Life*, where his wife had been offered a job as a doctor. In *Midway Upon the Journey of Our Life*, he presents this move as both an actualization of his marginalized status in Czechoslovak communist society and a gesture of self-exile, even self-chastisement. The title echoes the opening lines of Dante's *Inferno*, and like Dante, Jedlička – only in his late twenties – believes he has reached a moment of personal reckoning and reflection. He leads us into the 'hell' of 1950s north Bohemia, but unlike for Dante, there is no escape, no path to absolution and redemption. From the window of his flat in the Collective House, then internationally acclaimed as a paradigm of modern socialist architecture and now a listed monument, he forces himself to observe and record daily the catastrophic consequences of the ideology he once supported. The process of writing – and indeed reading – the text becomes an act of notionally endless atonement.

Though Jedlička had perhaps less to reproach himself for than his peers, *Midway Upon the Journey of Our Life* contains none of the self-justification and self-pity implicit in most comparable contemporaneous Czech and Slovak works. Early on, he refers sarcastically to his generation's naïve enthusiasm for the communist future. Like Kundera in *The Book of Laughter and Forgetting* (1979), he identifies the politically motivated execution in 1950 of the historian and literary theorist Záviš Kalandra as a key moment when young intellectuals should have woken up. Both Jedlička and, later, Kundera associate that 'waking-up' with a shift from the intoxication of lyric poetry to the sobriety of prose. For Jedlička, however, this shift is not so much a mark of personal maturity as an indicator of the spiritual decline of the times, encapsulated in the novella's closing travesty of the story of Daphnis and Chloe as a somewhat sordid encounter between an apprentice miner and a textile worker.

Among critics, interest has turned increasingly from the time of the text's publication to the time of writing, and its expression of the atmosphere of 1950s Bohemia. The Czech text is dedicated to 'Mr Wild', a reference to Václav Wild, a former Czechoslovak Communist who had left the Party in 1936, who became something of a father-figure to Jedlička. Their published correspondence does much to illuminate *Midway Upon the Journey of Our Life*, highlighting both the fractured, anxious interaction among marginalized intellectuals and their feverish search for a philosophical framework through which to understand their experience.

Jedlička's account radically contradicts the Party's characterization of life in north Bohemia in the period. Following the expulsion of most of the Bohemian German population after the Second World War, the region had acquired the status of 'virgin land', a tabula rasa on which the Czechoslovak Communist Party could realize Socialist paradise quickly and completely. The development of the region simultaneously marked the definitive Czech 're-conquering' of traditionally German-speaking territory ceded to Hitler's Germany through the 1938 Munich Agreement. Both aspects were highlighted in propaganda posters, exhibitions, literature and cinema, which contrasted the irrevocably inhuman, departing Bohemian Germans with the humane, in-coming Czechs, a fusion of national and socialist qualities.

As Jedlička describes, in practice the re-population brought together in a semi-lawless, impoverished postwar setting a diverse social and ethnic mix, including idealistic Communists, Czechs displaced to Eastern Europe during the war, Greeks fleeing their civil war, Hungarians, Ruthenians, Slovaks (including eastern Slovak Roma), and convicted criminals, broken families and other socially disadvantaged groups. Jedlička juxtaposes his blackly comic portrayal of the dysfunctional behaviour of his neighbours – their violence, selfishness, corruption and malevolence so at odds with the dreams of the architects of the Collective House – with chilling images of the brutal destruction of the landscape through rapid urbanization. Of particular note are the touching episodes featuring elderly people, whose post-war experience is often ignored in the rather self-centred work of their children's generation.

The first publication of *Midway Upon the Journey of Our Life* in the summer of 1966 coincided with an article in the prominent weekly newspaper *Literární noviny*, by Vladimír Karfík, which highlighted the major health, environmental and social problems in Most, the neighbouring town to Litvínov and a centre of open-cast mining of brown coal. Subsequent issues carried supportive letters from readers and responses from specialists. This relatively open and critical discussion reflected the growing liberalization in 1960s Czechoslovakia, further demonstrated by the positive critical response to Jedlička's book, which unquestionably captured the dominant intellectual mood of the time. The strength of Jedlička's withering critique, however, suggests that, unlike many contemporaries, he did not believe that this ideology and system could be reformed. Instead, *Midway Upon the Journey of Our Life* constitutes a fundamental attack on the broader utopian philosophy underlying the communist experiment, embodied in the bleak re-evocation of avant-garde techniques that gives the text its unique shape and style.

Typical of his intellectual generation, Jedlička grew up steeped in knowledge of Formalist and Structuralist theory (notably fostered during the inter-war period by Russian émigrés in the Prague Linguistic Circle), and the work of the 1920s and 1930s Czech Poetist and Surrealist avant-garde. In *Midway Upon the Journey of Our Life*, he mentions the leading Formalist theorist, Viktor Shklovsky, and reviewers quickly noticed the affinity between Jedlička's text and the 'literature of fact' propounded in 1920s Russia, above all by the LEF (Left Front of the Arts) group, to which Shklovsky belonged. LEF exhorted writers to abandon the bourgeois 'literature of invention' and immerse themselves in the apparently 'uninteresting' and 'everyday', and to participate in the construction of the new reality by documenting and analysing ever more closely the work in progress. Shklovsky's own practice in this area serves as a key model for *Midway Upon the Journey of Our Life*, above all Shklovsky's 1926 text *The Third Factory*, in which the author, who has seen the arrest, exile and execution of fellow intellectuals and whose theoretical positions face increasing marginalization and vilification, is haunted by 'guilty dreams'. At least in Shklovsky's hands, 'literature of fact' involves the disorientating switching of genres, including journalism, autobiography, memoir, story-telling and satire, and the replication of cinematic techniques in an attempt to capture dynamic, diffuse and unstable modernity (cf. Shklovsky's *Sentimental Journey: Memoirs 1917–1922* alluded to in Jedlička's book).

In *Midway Upon the Journey of Our Life*, Jedlička uses these methods to show how the avant-garde's utopian dreams of a new art for a new society were realized, paradigmatically in the northern Bohemian borderlands, in a dystopian art for a dystopian society and landscape. It seems only a defamiliarizing, Surrealist method can capture a society where everything is defamiliarized and surreal. The techniques of the avant-garde, conceived as a means of liberating the human being and restoring wholeness, meaning and energy to human existence, are used to express the imprisonment, alienation, meaninglessness and enforced apathy of post-revolutionary human existence. And Jedlička's narrator, an avant-garde writer, caught between the past and the future, writing for generations to come, no longer embodies pioneering heroism, but resembles the terrified northern Bohemian rabbit, trembling in the cold wind as its home is destroyed.

Since the fall of communism and Jedlička's death, *Midway Upon the Journey of Our Life* has belatedly come to be recognized in the Czech Republic as one of the most original and important works of Czech literature since 1945. It functions as both an unparalleled document of the social and intellectual crisis in 1950s Czechoslovakia and an extraordinary work of art, an encyclopaedia of the themes and preoccupations of Czech 1960s literature, whether personal confession, socio-political critique, absurd drama or formal experiment. In exile in West Germany in the 1970s and 1980s, Jedlička worked as an editor for Radio Free Europe, and his essays from this period repeatedly turn to the themes of courage, responsibility, authenticity and individuality familiar to international audiences from the work of Václav Havel. Yet unlike so much writing from this period, *Midway Upon the Journey of Our Life* has the capacity to live beyond its own historical context and address the philosophical, ecological and spiritual anxieties of our own times. In this respect alone, the precision of its testimony stands revealed.

Rajendra A. Chitnis   Bristol

Josef Jedlička's novella *Kde život náš je v půli se svou poutí /
Midway Upon the Journey of Our Life* is an extraordinary work
from a period of Czech literature that was inaccessible to
Czechs for nearly half a century, and to English speakers
remains almost entirely unknown. Founded in 1918, Czechoslovakia became a Communist country as the result of a
putsch by the Communist Party of Czechoslovakia, with
Soviet backing, in February 1948. Jedlička composed this
book in the years 1954–57, describing events from the end
of World War II to the time of its writing, a period known as
the Stalinist era, which in Czechoslovakia lasted even after
Stalin's death in 1953. It was the most brutal and repressive
time in the four decades of the CSSR's existence.

When I signed on to this project, I did so in the excited
belief that it would be the first work of Czech prose from
the 1950s to be translated into English. Turns out that isn't
true. But even if not unique in the way I first thought, it
is still one-of-a-kind as a literary work, casting a brighter,
starker light on certain aspects of Czech culture, politics,
and society than its predecessors and plunging into shadows
others have never even approached. For one thing, violence

by men—against women, against children, and against the environment—is rife throughout the text in a way I've never before encountered in Czech literature. This, together with Jedlička's critical view of the Communists' obsession with raising the standard of living (during the 1950s, an obsession as well in the countries on the other side of the Iron Curtain), suggests to me that Jedlička, even if he wouldn't have framed it in such terms, understood there to be a connection between patriarchy and the destruction of nature for economic gain. For another, the novella is not only a product of the Stalinist era, but equally strongly a product of World War II. Jedlička demonstrates the literally crushing impact of the war on human beings and their environment in one of *Midway Upon the Journey of Our Life*'s most vivid scenes, a bombing of the chemical refinery in Záluží by U.S. planes, along with its aftermath, both immediate—dead bodies and structural debris—and longer term, in the craters pocking the landscape, visited by children, years later, in search of plankton to feed their goldfish. Finally, as Rajendra Chitnis discusses in his afterword in detail, in writing this novella Jedlička was heavily influenced by the Russian writer and literary theorist Viktor Shklovsky. In short, whatever story Jedlička is trying to tell, he is also consciously creating an experimental work of art, placing form on an equal footing with content.

* * *

Due to the novella's unflinching portrayal of socialist society and its anything-but-socialist-realist style, it was out of the question for Jedlička to publish it at the time he wrote it. Again, as Rajendra Chitnis recounts, it was only in 1966, as censorship began to ease, that *Kde život náš je v půli se svou poutí* appeared in print, with the publishing house Československý spisovatel. A second, somewhat shorter version appeared in 1994, with Mladá fronta, incorporating changes Jedlička made just before his death in 1990. For my translation, Karolinum Press asked me to work from the critical edition, issued in 2010 by Host (together with Jedlička's sole novel, *Krev není voda / Blood Is Thicker Than Water*, first published by Československý spisovatel in 1991). The Host edition was edited by Emil and Marie Lukeš, who, in addition to stylistic revisions and structural changes, reinstated sections Jedlička had dropped for the second edition, making theirs the longest version of the book to have appeared in print.

In the course of my translation, I consulted with both Martin Janeček, the editor of the project for Karolinum Press, and Jakub Říha of the Institute of Czech Literature, who is familiar with all the existing editions of the Czech text. In response to some of my questions, Martin suggested I also refer to Erika Abrams's French translation, *Au milieu du chemin de notre vie* (Editions Noir sur Blanc, 2011). Abrams worked from the typewritten copy of Jedlička's original manuscript from the '50s, and prepared extensive endnotes, so in some cases her translation was helpful in clarifying the murkier parts of the text, or inconsistencies I noticed when it came to facts and chronology; in others, however, I could not rely on the French edition, since the text was substantially different from the version I was working from.

Given how rich with allusions and quotations *Midway Upon the Journey of Our Life* is, I considered supplementing my translation with notes as well. However, I discovered that most of the items I was inclined to annotate were not necessarily familiar to contemporary Czech readers either. This, combined with the availability of information via the internet, the fact that most readers find notes burdensome, and the publisher's decision to include a critical afterword, ultimately persuaded me that it was best to let the text stand on its own.

In closing I wish to offer thanks not only to Martin Janeček and Jakub Říha, whom I have already mentioned, and Rajendra Chitnis, for his insightful afterword, but also Ivana Husáková, who helped me deconstruct and interpret the most opaque sentences, and Petr Onufer, who first suggested the project to me. Finally, a warm PLAT shout-out to my fellow translators from the BILTC residency in summer 2014, where I did a substantial portion of my early work on this translation.

Alex Zucker

Brooklyn
January 2016

Josef Jedlička (1927–1990) was a Czech essayist and novelist. Expelled from Charles University in Prague after leaving the Communist Party, he moved to the border town of Litvínov, with his wife, a medical doctor, in 1953. In 1968, after the Soviet invasion and occupation of Czechoslovakia, he and his family emigrated to West Germany, where he worked as a cultural editor for Radio Free Europe in Munich. In addition to articles, studies, and reviews for Czech emigré journals, he wrote two works of fiction: the novella *Kde život náš je v půli se svou poutí* (*Midway Upon the Journey of Our Life*) and the novel *Krev není voda* (*Blood Is Thicker Than Water*). Most of his life he was banned from publishing in his native Czechoslovakia. His works have been translated into German, Italian, and French.

ABOUT THE TRANSLATOR

Alex Zucker (b. 1964) has translated novels by Jáchym Topol, Petra Hůlová, Patrik Ouředník, Heda Margolius Kovály, Tomáš Zmeškal, and Magdaléna Platzová. He is winner of an English PEN Award for Writing in Translation, an NEA Literary Fellowship, and the ALTA National Translation Award. In addition to translating, he has worked in journalism and human rights. From 1990 to 1995 he lived in Prague, and he currently lives in Brooklyn, New York.